Was it so wrong to want to kiss Max good-night?

Miranda knew how his lips would feel on hers—warm and firm.

He crossed the room, lifted her up and carried her up the stairs. With her arms around his neck, her cheek was pressed against his.

"Max," she gasped, "I'm too much for you."

"You're right," he said, backing onto her feather bed and cradling her tightly to him. "Way too much." He rolled onto his back, cushioning her and sinking deeper into the soft billows of the bed, one arm around her shoulders, the other on her round bottom. She turned to roll out of his arms and landed on top of him, her bandaged foot in the air, feeling ridiculous, but so relaxed and mellow she didn't care.

"Come here," he muttered.

"Where?" she asked. But she knew. . . .

Dear Reader,

Blue skies, sunshine, the scent of fresh-cut grass, a walk on the shore—some summer pleasures are irresistible. And Silhouette Romance has six more to add to your list—this month's irresistible heroes who will light up your August days—or nights—with romance!

He may act like a man of steel, but this FABULOUS FATHER has a heart of gold. Years of separation had made Gavin Hunter a stranger to his son, yet he was determined to make his home with the boy. But with beautiful Norah Bennett standing in his way, could Gavin win his son's heart without losing his own? Find out in Lucy Gordon's *Instant Father*.

Our next hero can be found in Elizabeth August's own SMYTHESHIRE, MASSACHUSETTS. Ryder Gerard may have married Emily Sayer to protect her young son, but he never intended to fall in love. *A Wedding for Emily* weaves the mysterious legacy of Smytheshire with the magic of marital love.

No reader will be able to resist the rugged, enigmatic Victor Damien. In Stella Bagwell's *Hero in Disguise,* reporter Sabrina Martin sets out to discover what her sexy boss, Victor, has to hide. Sabrina always gets her story, but will she get her man?

For more wonderful heroes to spend these lazy summer days with, check out Carol Grace's *Mail-Order Male,* Joan Smith's *John Loves Sally* and exciting new author Pamela Dalton's *The Prodigal Husband*.

In the coming months, we'll be bringing you books by all your favorite authors, such as Diana Palmer, Annette Broadrick, Marie Ferrarella, Carla Cassidy and many more.

Happy reading!

Anne Canadeo
Senior Editor

MAIL-ORDER MALE
Carol Grace

Silhouette
ROMANCE™
Published by Silhouette Books New York
America's Publisher of Contemporary Romance

SILHOUETTE BOOKS
300 East 42nd St., New York, N.Y. 10017

MAIL-ORDER MALE

Copyright © 1993 by Carol Culver

All rights reserved. Except for use in any review, the reproduction or utilization of this work in whole or in part in any form by any electronic, mechanical or other means, now known or hereafter invented, including xerography, photocopying and recording, or in any information storage or retrieval system, is forbidden without the permission of the publisher, Silhouette Books, 300 E. 42nd St., New York, N.Y. 10017

ISBN: 0-373-08955-4

First Silhouette Books printing August 1993

All the characters in this book have no existence outside the imagination of the author and have no relation whatsoever to anyone bearing the same name or names. They are not even distantly inspired by any individual known or unknown to the author, and all incidents are pure invention.

®: Trademark used under license and registered in the United States Patent and Trademark Office and in other countries.

Printed in the U.S.A.

CAROL GRACE

has always been interested in travel and living abroad. She spent her junior year in college in France and toured the world working on the hospital ship *Hope*. She and her husband spent the first year and a half of their marriage in Iran where they both taught English. Then, with their toddler daughter, they lived in Algeria for two years.

Carol says that writing is another way of making her life exciting. Her office is an Airstream trailer parked behind her mountaintop home, which overlooks the Pacific Ocean. She shares her home with her inventor husband, their teenage daughter and their twelve-year-old son.

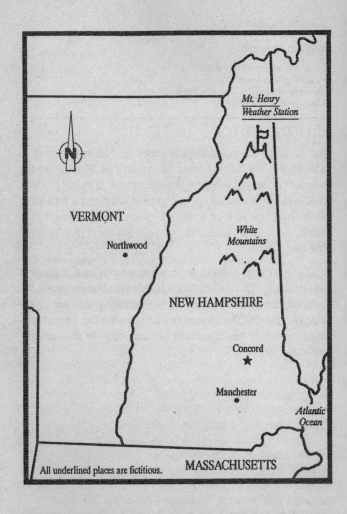

Mt. Henry
Weather Station

VERMONT

Northwood

White
Mountains

NEW HAMPSHIRE

Concord

Manchester

Atlantic
Ocean

All underlined places are fictitious.

MASSACHUSETTS

Chapter One

Miranda Morrison peered hopefully into the depths of the plastic gallon bucket, but it was dry. Pressing her head against the bark of the giant red maple, she swore under her breath. Damn, double damn, not a trace of sap, and here it was mid-March. No sense in even checking the other pails on the other trees. If Big Red didn't produce, there wasn't much hope for the rest of them. Mud oozed over the toes of her black rubber boots as she plodded back to the house to change her clothes. Good thing she didn't count on the farm for her living. Good thing she had a job in town, or she'd have to sell the farm.

It wasn't the best job in town, she reflected as she maneuvered her old pickup truck down the two-lane road, it was the *only* job in town. Northwood was a company town and she worked for the company—Green Mountain Mail-Order Merchants. Her job was not only to handle customer complaints, but to pose for the catalog pictures, along with most of the other employees under the age of sixty-five. She hadn't been there all that long, but sometimes it seemed as if it were an eternity. It was just that she didn't want to work for anybody but herself. If she could only spend all of her time on the farm, then she'd see some progress, wouldn't she?

As Miranda drove, she noticed that the snow was disappearing as fast as her hopes for a good sapping season, taking with it chunks of the road. She swerved to avoid a giant pothole and missed. The next thing she knew there was a jarring thud and she was leaning at a forty-five-degree angle, the front left wheel of her truck lodged in the pothole.

Gingerly she examined herself for injuries and found none. She slid out from under the wheel and stood on the deserted road, staring at her lopsided truck. Why hadn't she allowed time for these mishaps, which happened all too frequently? She couldn't be late, not again. But after pacing back and forth on the slick road for ten minutes, she got lucky. Howard Tucker came along and pulled her out with the winch and pulley he always carried in the back of his Jeep.

"Thanks, Howard," she said, back in the driver's seat again. "I owe you one."

He waved his hand, dismissing the thought. "Pay me back in syrup."

She sighed, closing the door and rolling down the window. "I wish I could. But I'm afraid we might not have much of a season this year."

He ambled closer. "Ever think about selling the old place?"

"Not really. What would you want it for anyway? You've already got eighty acres of your own."

He shrugged. "Just thought I'd take it off your hands. Seems a shame, you burying yourself way out there. Must get lonely after being in the big city."

She shook her head. "I like it. It's home." She didn't tell him it was more than just home. It was a safe haven, a refuge where she could be herself, maybe even support herself one day. She looked at her watch and grimaced inwardly. "Thanks again."

Miranda sped into town and the Green Mountain Mail-Order Merchants parking lot only fifteen minutes late, raced into the building, threw her jacket on the coatrack and stopped just long enough to fill her cup with coffee in the linoleum-tiled lunchroom. Then she hurried to her desk in a tiny cubbyhole, which was next to four other desks in four identical cubbyholes that made up the complaints department. A quick glance told her she wasn't the only one who was late. In fact, she was the only one there so far.

Before she attacked the pile of yellow complaint forms on her desk, she looked over her shoulder. There was no time clock, not yet. But there *was* old Mr. Northwood, who always padded through the knotty-pine offices in his rubber-soled duck-hunting shoes, looking for those workers who didn't embody the Vermont work ethic. But not today. Apparently he was late, too. Relieved, she turned back to her desk, noticing that her voice mail was overflowing and eight of the ten incoming lines were flashing urgent orange signals.

"Good morning, Green Mountain Merchants," she said eight times, and then, "Will you hold?" They all said yes, except for number eight, who wouldn't hold, wouldn't even consider it.

"I've been *holding* for twenty minutes, since nine o'clock, listening to a recorded message telling me to call between nine and five. I guess I should be grateful you people come to work at all," he said in a deep sarcastic voice with just a tinge of a Southern accent.

Miranda took a deep breath. "How can I help you, Mr...."

"Carter. Maxwell Randolph Carter."

She watched the orange lights on her phone console flash, imagining seven angry people hanging up, redialing and getting the recorded message all over again. "What can I do for you, Mr. Carter?"

"You can call me Max and then you can get my all-weather boots up here. Do you know how long I've been waiting for those boots?"

She grabbed a sack of already-processed customer forms and frantically thumbed through them. "Uh, no...no I don't, but I can assure you..."

"That they'll be here tomorrow, I know, that's what they always say."

"Have we talked before?" she asked, knowing fully well that if she *had* heard that voice before, she'd have remembered the slight drawl, which she might have found irresistible, but which under the present circumstances, she found quite resistible.

"I may have talked to you, ma'am. I don't know. I've lost count. I assume you work in the complaint department and that you handle complaints when you're not too busy, although I don't know your name."

"Miranda Morrison," she said as politely as she could through clenched teeth. Her fingers flew through the stack of papers and her eyes lit on his order at last. "Here we have it," she said reassuringly. "*Aha.* The boots *have* been sent. That was two weeks ago. You should have them by now."

"I know they've been sent. But they haven't been received. That's the problem. What are you going to do about it?"

"We're going to make everything right. That's our policy and our philosophy. Now let me have your address again, just so we get it right. Can you wait just a minute?" Knowing he'd probably say no, she put him on hold without waiting for an answer and went to the other lines, praying they were easier problems. But the first was a woman who wanted to know how to refill her plastic bird feeder.

Miranda flipped through the winter catalog and found it on page thirteen. She turned the picture upside down, but she still couldn't figure out how to fill it. *If only someone else would show up and take some of these calls!* She put the woman on hold and went back to Maxwell Carter.

"Where were you?" he demanded.

"I had another call, something urgent," she explained.

"More urgent than a man in three feet of new snow without boots?"

"It's about a bird feeder." She looked around nervously. The Northwoods hated it when the conversation deviated from the order at hand in any way. She suspected they listened in randomly on her and the others.

"What about the bird feeder?" he asked.

"She doesn't know how to fill it. She's trying to pry the suction cups off the glass."

"Maybe I can help. Is it the one on page thirteen in your winter catalog?"

"Yes, it is."

"Tell her to slide the tray out."

"I was just going to do that, but I didn't want to keep you waiting."

There was a sound that was a cross between a snort and a chuckle. "I'll wait," he said.

In less than a minute she was back on the line with him. "Thank you. The woman was very grateful to you."

"You told her about me?" he asked, faint surprise in the deep voice.

"There wasn't much to tell, except that you're bootless in three feet of snow. Now if I can have your address . . ."

"Is that you holding the bird feeder?" he asked abruptly.

Miranda tapped her knuckles against her desk, praying someone wasn't listening to them in the back office. "No, that's Mavis Lund. I'm on page eighteen, in the thermal underwear." Belatedly she heard the pages turning on the other end of the line and she felt the color flood her face. What was wrong with her, exposing her body to a total stranger? Yes, the underwear was double-ply, but it was one piece from head to toe and it did cling in certain places. Drat the Northwoods for being too penny-pinching to hire real models! There was a long silence and she thought she heard a quick, sharp intake of breath.

"Is that what you're wearing right now?"

"This is what everyone is wearing now," she said briskly, "under their clothes until the end of winter, and if you're in three feet of snow, I suggest you order a pair of men's underwear from the next page." Anything to get his mind off her picture.

"Fine. Throw one in."

She grabbed an original order blank. "Size?"

"Extra large."

"And now your work address."

"Mount Henry, New Hampshire, home of the world's worst weather."

"What are you, a park ranger?" she asked, scribbling furiously.

"Meteorologist. Every three hours I go outside and read the instruments at six-thousand feet."

"Isn't a six-thousand foot climb a bit much to ask of a mailman?"

"All I ask is that *you* send the boots by express mail. The mailman brings them to the ranger station at the bottom of the mountain and the ranger brings them up in the Sno-Cat," he explained with exaggerated patience. "It's a very good system, foolproof. Until now, that is."

Ignoring the implication that somebody at the company was a fool, she promised she'd send another pair of boots that very morning, and that if he didn't get them the next day, she'd come up there personally and deliver them. As soon as she said the words, however, she knew the North-woods would never approve such a plan, despite their "customer is always right" policy. But why worry about something that would never happen?

"Will you bring them up in your long underwear?" he asked.

"Absolutely," she promised airily, certain that now she had fed Maxwell Carter's name into the computer the boots were as good as in his hands, or on his feet. Then she said goodbye and proceeded to clear all the other lines by taking care of the remaining problems in record time, exchanging sweaters, making adjustments in shoes, jackets and flannel-shirt orders. And after that she went back to the warehouse, ordered another pair of boots and slapped the preprinted label on the package. But instead of trusting the mail room, she walked down Main Street to the post office, where she said goodbye to the boots and to Mr. Maxwell Carter forever.

On slushy sidewalks she trudged back toward the three-story brick building that dominated the town, sidestepping pools of muddy water. New Englanders called it the mud, the season between winter and spring, and for good reason. Of course, she wouldn't care if the mud came up to the top of her boots if the sap would run. If the sap would run she'd make syrup, and if she made syrup, she'd sell it and when she sold it . . .

"Miranda." Her sister Ariel grabbed her by the arm. "I was looking all over the office for you. Are we having lunch today or what?"

Miranda looked into the round blue eyes of her older sister, surprised to find it was noon already. Together they headed back down Main Street toward Simpson's Diner.

"Where were you?" her sister asked when they were sitting across from each other in a booth.

"At the post office, rushing an order to a customer."

"Must be pretty special if he rates a trip to the post office," Ariel said with a hopeful gleam in her eye.

Miranda pulled her gloves off and looked at the menu. "*He* thinks he's special because he works outside in three feet of snow *and* he expects me to drop everything and rush his boots to him— Oh, no." She slapped her palm against her forehead. "I forgot to send the pair of long underwear he ordered. Knowing him, he'll complain to Mr. Northwood next."

The waitress came by and Ariel ordered the clam chowder and half a sandwich before asking, "What do you mean, 'knowing him'? How well do you know him?"

Miranda told the waitress she'd have the same, then turned her attention to her sister's probing gaze.

"I don't know him at all, but I told him I'd deliver the boots in person if they don't get there tomorrow."

"How exciting. Is he married?"

Miranda leaned back against the vinyl padding of the booth and sighed. "How should I know? I suppose you would have asked him?"

"There are ways. You could have said, 'What about a pair of boots for your wife?' Or, 'Will there be someone home, your wife maybe, to sign for the package?' "

Miranda shook her head in awe. "Honestly, sometimes I wonder how your mind works. I don't have the time or energy to delve into the personal lives of the customers, especially not today. Donna and Mavis are out sick. Penny's son has chicken pox and Lianne's at the dentist. So I've had a lot of complaints today, all theirs and mine, too, but his was the worst, he was the most insistent.... And then he had the nerve to call me *ma'am*." She bit into her sandwich and chewed vigorously.

"I wonder why he called you ma'am."

"Probably because he's from the South."

Ariel cocked her head to one side. "What's his name, anyway, or did you forget to ask?"

"Carter, Maxwell Randolph Carter."

Ariel licked her spoon and gazed dreamily past Miranda. "From an old aristocratic family, I'll bet, with a mansion just dripping with magnolias."

"We're from an old family. We go back to the revolutionary war."

"Only we had icicles dripping from our house," Ariel reminded her.

"I remember Grandma wouldn't let us keep them in the freezer for the summer. She made us throw them out."

"I don't know how Grandma and Grandpa managed. And we weren't even their own kids. We just got dumped on their doorstep."

Miranda sighed. "I wish I'd had a chance to tell them I was coming back."

Ariel squeezed her hand. "They knew you would."

"Did they ever have a sapping season when there was no sap?"

Ariel shook her head. "Never. Just be patient. Conditions aren't right yet. Temperatures have to drop below freezing at night and then warm up during the day."

Miranda frowned. "I'm counting on the sap."

Her sister leaned forward. "Miranda, don't count on the sap. Find a man and count on *him.*"

"Like you did."

"Yes, and then when things go wrong at work and someone yells at you or the sap doesn't run, you've got somebody to lean on and a shoulder to cry on. That's what husbands are for. And if anybody needs one, you do."

Finished with their food, they laid their money in the little plastic tray provided on top of the check on their table and walked out the door. "That sounds like a song I heard on the radio this morning. Why don't you quit your job in the retail outlet and write the words to country music?" Miranda asked teasingly.

Ariel shook her head, taking her sister's words seriously. "No, I don't think so. I need to get out of the house for a few hours every day. Besides, I like it in the store. People from New York come in and they think everything's so quaint and rustic. Then when I go home to the kids and Rob

I forget about it. Why don't you ask to transfer? You need to get out of that cubbyhole and meet some people. Normal people, who have no complaints.''

Miranda tossed her scarf over her shoulder. "I've already met enough New Yorkers. That's why I left the city, so I wouldn't have to meet any more of them."

Ariel slanted a long, sympathetic glance in her direction. "You can't blame the whole population for what happened to you."

"I don't blame anyone but myself. I shouldn't have ever gone to the city. You warned me. But I guess I had to find out for myself." Miranda felt a chill that had nothing to do with the wind blowing up the street. No matter how unpleasant things got back in complaints, she'd never been mugged or harassed or burglarized in Northwood, and she probably never would.

"I'm sorry it didn't work out," Ariel said, "but I'm glad you came home. For two years I had no one to eat lunch with, no one to leave the kids with..."

"No one to nag about getting out and getting married."

Her sister grinned and they parted at the front door of Green Mountain Merchants. Ariel turned right, to the retail outlet, and Miranda went back to her desk to solve more problems. But in between calls she thought about the man without the boots. She filed his order under unsolved mysteries and shoved it to the back of the drawer, but the sound of his voice came back to her, the way he rounded off his consonants and hung onto his vowels. He had the accent all right, but he was no Southern gentleman. Maybe he'd been up north too long, long enough to lose any Southern charm he'd arrived with.

Disgusted with herself for daydreaming, she turned on her answering machine at precisely five o'clock and went to get her jacket. Maybe Ariel was right, maybe she did need to get out and meet people. But what people? She already knew everyone in town. On the way home she prayed for cold weather, cold enough to make the sap run so she could make a living selling syrup and she'd never have to deal with irate customers or work for anyone again.

A hundred and twenty miles to the northeast, Max Carter scanned the sky from the weather station on top of Mount Henry. The wind blew across the rooftop observation deck, nowhere near the record two hundred and thirty miles per hour, but strong enough to knock all six feet three inches of him down to his knees as he tried to read the barometer. He picked himself up and braced his hands against the railing. This wouldn't have happened if he'd had his new boots with the rubber chain-tread outsole on.

Ice built up on his goggles until he could hardly see. He couldn't blame that on Miranda Morrison of Green Mountain Merchants, but just about everything else he could. He couldn't stay outside long enough to take accurate readings, that was her fault. He couldn't walk without sliding in the snow, that was her fault. And he couldn't concentrate on fixing the broken psychometric calculator, that was *definitely* her fault. He stomped inside the observatory, removed three outer layers of clothes and hung them to dry next to the stove.

Of course, it might help his concentration to put away the Green Mountain Merchants catalog, or at least turn the page so he wouldn't have to look at her picture anymore. He had to admit, it surprised him. Talking to her, he'd expected a little pinched face with rimless glasses and hair pulled tight in a bun. But she looked like an advertisement for health food instead of long underwear. He sat in his swivel chair, propped his stocking-clad feet on his desk between his computer and the shortwave radio and looked at her picture again.

Blond hair in a...what did they call it...a French braid? Wide brown eyes and pink cheeks. Not a trace of makeup, as if she'd just gotten up or was just going to bed. The long johns weren't sexy, but she sure was, with high, full breasts, a narrow waist and long slender legs.

Dream on, he told himself. You picked the wrong kind of job for that kind of woman. Or any kind. Women liked to have their men around, not just half time, but all the time. Otherwise they got lonely and started looking around. You couldn't blame them for that. He had once, but not anymore.

He hoped the weather would clear tomorrow so Fred could get up the road in the Sno-Cat. Not only would he bring the boots, but he'd also bring fresh food. That's what he needed, hush puppies and crab cakes, not a call from a cool, unfeeling clerk with the face of an angel and the body of Venus in long underwear.

The next morning he ate the last of his bacon for breakfast. He called Fred at noon after a long morning trying to track the altocumulus clouds that were breaking up. "Mail come yet?"

"Yep. You got a bill from Green Mountain Merchants."

"A *bill?*" He felt the back of his neck burn. "Is that all?"

"Nope. You got a postcard from Florida, want me to read it?"

"No, thanks. Is that all?"

"That's it."

"Looks like it's going to clear today. What time are you coming up?"

"'Bout three, I guess, unless I hear from Ellie. The baby isn't due for another week, but you never know. You sure about the weather? Because I wouldn't want to get stuck up there."

"No guarantees, but it looks good right now. Don't forget the box of food from New Orleans labeled Perishable."

"The UPS people put it right in the tractor."

Max hung up and dialed again. It was just past twelve. She'd probably be at lunch. She'd probably be at lunch for hours, knowing her. He braced himself for a recording. After an eternity a human voice answered, but it wasn't hers. He was momentarily speechless. Should he explain the situation to this person, or should he ask for Ms. Morrison, or should he hang up and try again? He opened his mouth. "This is Maxwell Carter—"

"Just a moment," the voice interrupted.

"Don't put me on hold," he ordered, but she did. The next voice he heard was Miranda's. When he told her the boots hadn't arrived, she said she was sorry and then there was a long silence.

"Are you sure they didn't get there?" she asked.

"Positive. The bill got here, though. You had no problem getting *that* here on time."

"That wasn't me, that was accounting."

"That explains it."

There was a short pause and he pictured her bent over her desk, her blond hair escaping from the braid and cascading down her back and over her long underwear.

"As you know, Green Mountain guarantees satisfaction." Her voice jolted him back to reality.

With the portable phone in his hand he walked to the window and looked out at the snow-covered mountains in the distance. "So they say."

"They don't just say it, they mean it." She cleared her throat. "So... I intend to deliver your boots to you this afternoon, or rather to the ranger station if that's acceptable."

"You have to be here by three o'clock."

"I'll be there if the weather holds."

"It will. Uh... Ms. Morrison?"

"Yes?"

"Drive carefully."

"Don't worry. If anything happens to me, your boots are fully insured."

"If anything happens to you, would someone else take your place?"

"Yes, so you see, you can't lose either way."

"Right."

Miranda hung up and ran her fingers through her hair. She took her headset off and confided in Donna, who'd gone to high school with her and now occupied the cubbyhole next to hers. As she always did, Donna told her exactly what she wanted to hear. That she had no choice but to requisition another pair of all-weather boots and a pair of double-ply men's long underwear—which she'd forgotten to send yesterday, anyway—and drive to New Hampshire. She, Donna, would cover for Miranda the way Miranda had covered for her the day her son was in the nursery school play.

Still, Miranda wouldn't have considered leaving early if Mr. Northwood were breathing down her neck, but he was home with the flu. So she slipped into the warehouse, thinking that in a few hours she'd have delivered the package and would be on her way back, leaving behind a satisfied customer. And maybe she'd even solve the mystery of the two pairs of missing boots while she was there.

With the package under her arm, she stopped by the pine-paneled outlet on her way out. Ariel was wrapping a hand-knit cardigan for a customer. When she finished, she regarded her sister with openmouthed surprise. "Where are you going so early?"

"I'm going to deliver the boots to the customer I was telling you about yesterday. Donna's covering for me."

Ariel rubbed her hands together in excitement. "How far south is it?"

"He's *from* the South, not *in* the South. He works on top of Mount Henry, in the world's worst weather, which is why he needs the boots so badly."

"How old is this man?" Ariel asked with a puzzled frown.

"I don't know, and I'm afraid I never will because I will leave the boots at the ranger station and the ranger will take them up the mountain with the mail in a Sno-Cat and unless there's an avalanche the boots will be delivered and I'll never ever hear from Maxwell Randolph Carter again." She drew a deep breath while Ariel directed a customer toward a rack of quilts.

"Keep this to yourself," Miranda cautioned. "I don't want this to get back to the management."

Her sister raised her right hand. "On my honor. But couldn't you just ask the ranger how old Mr. Carter is and if he's married?"

Half exasperated, but knowing her sister would never give up, Miranda set her package on the counter and buttoned her jacket. "I'll see what I can do— Oh, my Lord, I forgot the long underwear again. Have you got a pair of men's extra large back there?"

Ariel turned to the shelves behind her. "I think so, but are you sure that's the right size?"

"That's what he said."

Ariel held the underwear up, her arms stretched out as wide as they'd go. Miranda's eyes moved from shoulder to shoulder, across the itch-free cotton. "Could he be that large?" Ariel asked, biting her lip anxiously.

Miranda threw her hands in the air. "I don't know. Maybe he looks like the Incredible Hulk. Put it in a bag. I've got to get going." She waved to her sister over her shoulder, left the building, got into her truck and headed onto the Interstate. The weather stayed clear and cold, just as he'd said, and she arrived at the ranger station with minutes to spare. There was a Sno-Cat parked outside the door and she ran her gloved hand over the treads.

"How do you like her?" A male voice came from behind her. She turned. A man in a down jacket and a hat with flaps over the ears smiled proudly at the shiny machine.

"Great. I've got a tractor at home. A little older and a little worse for wear. The clutch went out last summer."

"They do that when they get old. This one here's probably a lot like yours, just newer."

"Are you the ranger? I've got a package for Mr. Carter, the meteorologist."

"Yep. You can put it inside with the food and the rest of the mail. He'll be glad to see you. Nobody's been up for a week, and he's running low on fresh food. I started up last Monday, but had to turn back because of the fog."

"Oh, no, I'm not going up. I'm just delivering the package. Mr. Carter said to leave it here." She glanced up at the snow-packed road that wound up the mountain.

"Up to you." The ranger looked her over. "Can't believe he told you just to leave it. Does he know you very well?"

"Not at all. I mean, just on the phone." She pulled her hat down over her ears. "Have you worked here long?"

"Me? About five years. Max has only been here over a year. Came up from someplace in Georgia."

"I thought maybe he'd be retiring soon," she said, feeling shameless.

"Retiring, at thirty-two?"

"Oh, no, of course not." She took a deep breath and gathered her courage. "It must be hard on wives being separated from their husbands...."

Fred nodded vigorously. "You can say that again. My wife doesn't even want me driving up there, for fear I might get stuck and not get down, especially now— Is that the phone?"

He turned and disappeared into the small concrete structure that housed the station. Miranda opened the door to the tractor and climbed in. She put the box in the back of the vehicle, and then, unable to resist, sat on the comfortable padded seat, pushing the gas pedal and working the gearshift through its four positions. As soon as she had the money, she'd get her tractor fixed, before summer, if possible, so she could put in some barley.

She looked up to see Fred knocking frantically on the windshield. "Oh, miss, I've got to go. My wife's in labor. Could you just slide the keys in the ashtray?"

Miranda opened the side window to answer, but he was gone. Somewhere in the distance she heard a car start, wheels squeal and then she saw him drive past her, waving with one hand and steering with the other. For several moments she sat staring out the windshield at the mountains in front of her. She'd been driving tractors since she was fifteen, but never a Sno-Cat. She'd always wanted to drive one, but never had the chance. She had no doubt she could drive it on open flat ground, but up a snow-covered mountain road?

She could see there were markers on either side of the road, and she wouldn't run into any traffic. On the other hand she had fulfilled her responsibility. She'd delivered the boots to the ranger station. It wasn't her fault if the ranger had a more important delivery to attend to. Max Carter couldn't blame her this time. Or could he?

She looked at the boxes behind her in the cab. Cartons of groceries, and a shoe box full of mail. No packages from Green Mountain. Where were all those boots? Was it true he was running out of supplies? Was he irritable because he was hungry? Miranda pressed her hand against her stomach and heard it growl in sympathy.

She turned the key in the ignition and the engine roared to life. Her pulse quickened. It might be her only chance to ever drive a Sno-Cat. She'd deliver the goods and come right back down, and she'd still be home this evening. Fred would understand. He might have even suggested it if he hadn't left so suddenly. And Maxwell Carter would be grateful to her for life. She'd not only save him from wet feet, but she'd also save him from starvation.

She smiled to herself and eased the big tractor onto the steep road. The wide cleats gripped firmly and she took the first turn with ease. She laughed aloud. This was fun. She took the next turn and the next, hardly noticing the small wisps of fog that swirled by the windows. With one final roar, she reached the summit and saw a small concrete building built on a platform above her. She cut the engine and jumped out, so flushed with exhilaration she scarcely realized that the fog was thicker now, cold and damp and blowing in her face.

The dark form of a man came toward her, shouting Fred's name.

"I'm not Fred," she shouted back.

He loomed over her, a shock of dark blond hair blown across his forehead, and gripped her tightly by the arms. "Get inside. We'll get the boxes later."

She shook her head and her teeth chattered. "I can't stay. I'm going back."

He pulled her toward the building, now barely visible in the icy fog. "No, you're not. Whoever you are, you're not leaving."

Miranda was never sure how she got up the stairs to the one-room observation tower, but she knew she'd never been happier to be inside anywhere in her life. It was warm, it was bright and it was dry. She pulled her hat off and her hair tumbled to her shoulders. She stood in the middle of the room, panting from the climb up the ladder, and stared at the man across the room who was staring at her.

"You certainly aren't Fred," he said.

"Miranda Morrison, from Green Mountain."

His eyes traveled the length of her black stretch pants to her lined boots and back up to her face. "I didn't recognize you with your clothes on."

She felt the heat rise to her face. "I brought the boots. They're in the tractor."

"Where's Fred?"

"He couldn't make it. His wife's having a baby."

"So he told you to drive up here by yourself?" Max was still staring at her as if she'd materialized out of the mist, although he was quite sure she was flesh and blood.

"It was my idea," she confessed. "You said you needed the boots. He said you needed food."

She looked as if she needed food herself, this woman who'd just driven a two-ton tractor up a mountain in the fog. She looked as if she were going to keel over if he didn't do something fast. "Sit down." He pointed to the daybed in the corner and he was glad he'd taken the time to drape it with the brown plaid cover it came with. She sat down gingerly, as if she were afraid it would collapse under her, and he saw her gaze sweep over his desk in the corner, scattered with papers, books and, in the middle, the Green Mountain catalog. She turned her head toward the window that faced east and regarded what would have been an awesome view of the White Mountains if it hadn't been for the fog.

He crossed the room and went to the built-in shelves above his desk, casually shoving the catalog under a stack of papers. "What can I get you, a brandy, some sherry? I usually have a drink before dinner. It's a little early, but under the circumstances..."

"Nothing, thanks," she said, straightening her spine. "I've got a long drive ahead of me."

With a glass in one hand and a bottle in the other, he paused. "No, you don't. I thought I mentioned that you couldn't leave. Not tonight. There's fog out there so thick you could cut it with a knife."

"Oh, but I have to leave tonight. Right now, before it gets dark."

"Is someone expecting you, your husband?"

"No."

"No, you don't have a husband, or no, he isn't expecting you?"

"I don't have a husband, but there are people who will worry if I don't get back."

He poured two glasses of an old mellow sherry he'd been saving for some special occasion. "Who?"

"My sister."

He handed her the glass of amber liquid. "You can call her. Tell her there's zero visibility and that you're safe." He watched her eyes narrow as she looked him over. "You are safe," he assured her, taking the swivel chair and straddling it. "I'm not a sex maniac or a serial killer."

A nervous smile played at the corner of her mouth. "How do I know that?"

"I've got letters of recommendation from respectable scientists and even one from the president of the American Chess Association."

She pulled the zipper of her jacket up to her chin. "Some of the most devious people in the world are chess players."

"Are you?"

"What, devious?"

"No, a chess player."

"Yes, but I'm not very good at it."

He felt the sherry slide down the back of his throat. "We'll see after dinner."

"Dinner?"

"You didn't think I'd let you starve, did you?" He stood up and handed her the phone. "Call your sister and I'll go get the stuff."

"You have a telephone all the way up here?"

"A phone and a shortwave radio for emergencies. All the comforts of home."

Miranda held the telephone in her hands. Out of the corner of her eye she could see Max's dark blond head bending over to snap his boots on, his old worn rubber boots. She wanted to wait until he left to call, but she had nothing else to do, no reason to put it off except she didn't want him listening in on her conversation.

She punched in the numbers slowly. "Listen, Ariel, I'm stuck in some bad weather so I won't be back till later."

"Morning," Max said from across the room. "At least until morning."

"Where are you? Who's that with you?"

"I'm at the weather station and that's the weatherman."

"If he's the weatherman, how come he didn't know about this bad weather?"

"I'll ask him that. And I'll be back tomorrow." Whatever happened she didn't want Ariel to worry. She'd gotten herself into this mess and she'd get herself out.

"You're spending the night with the weatherman?" Ariel's voice went up a notch. "You don't even know him."

"That's right, but I have no choice. I'm fogged in on top of Mount Henry."

"Well, is he really extra large?"

Miranda's gaze wandered to the tall man with the very broad shoulders who was putting his jacket on at the door. He was large all right. But she couldn't tell her sister that. "Uh... I'll talk to you tomorrow. Bye now." She handed the phone back to Max. "Can I help bring in the boxes?"

He shook his head. "Take off your jacket and boots. Turn up the heat and make yourself at home. When I get the food in here, we'll talk about dinner." A rush of cold wind blew in before he slammed the door after him.

Miranda stood in the middle of the room, staring at the heavy storm door. She was stuck overnight in a forty-foot square room with huge windows on four sides, storage cabinets and a desk, but with no visible kitchen or bathroom. The man seemed harmless, but how could she tell? She had no instincts for judging men, that was Ariel's specialty. What would they do here until dark, and more important, what would they do *after* dark? She gave a little shiver as the wind and fog swirled around the building. And braced herself for a long winter's evening.

Chapter Two

"You've got some questions to answer."

Miranda whirled around at the sound of his voice. She'd taken off her jacket and her boots, turned up the heat and taken herself on a tour of Maxwell Carter's weather station, from the tiny kitchen hidden behind a wall of shelves to the bathroom that looked like a storage closet. She'd just taken a sip of her sherry when he suddenly appeared at the door. Setting her glass on a table, she hurried to take the top two boxes from the stack he was carrying. She followed him through the narrow doorway to the kitchen, set the boxes down and looked up inquisitively. "Questions?"

Max surveyed her from the top of her honey-blond hair to her lightweight hiking boots, his eyes lingering on the baggy oatmeal sweater that only hinted at the curves underneath, and forced himself to think about dinner. A subject that had been uppermost on his mind until he saw her get out of the tractor. Now his mind was preoccupied with questions he wanted to ask her. First, was she really wearing long underwear? If so, it must be very thin and very formfitting, and he knew exactly how she'd look in it after studying the catalog so carefully.

Inwardly shaking his head to clear his thoughts, he said, "Questions? Oh, yes. What do you like, crayfish *étouffée* or shrimp gumbo?" He stacked the boxes on the counter and slit open the one on top.

She leaned over to read the label. "Louisiana Seafood. You weren't kidding. You're really going to make one of those things."

"Of course. You didn't think meteorologists lived like savages, did you?"

"I didn't really think about them at all until a few days ago, and now..."

"And now you wish you'd never heard of them. Which brings me to question number two. Why in God's name did you take it into your head to drive up here in a Sno-Cat by yourself?"

She pressed her hands together and lowered her eyes. "I don't know, except that I have a tractor at home and I thought I could do it. So I just did. I had no idea this would happen. You said the weather was clear." She threw a glance in the direction of the window and the fog that swirled just outside the glass. "If you're a weatherman, how come you didn't know about this fog?"

"I did know about it. I called Fred to tell him not to come up, but he didn't answer, then his line was busy and then no answer. When I talked to you at noon there was no fog. It was clear from here to Vermont."

She stared at the window in disbelief. "Can you really see that far?"

"Farther. If it clears up in the morning, I'll show you."

Now it was her turn to look him over with narrowed eyes, and he had the feeling she was still trying to decide whether to stay or not, despite what he'd told her.

He exhaled loudly. "Look, Ms. Morrison... Miranda, you're stuck here for the night, whether you like it or not. I didn't ask you to come up here. Okay, maybe I wanted to see if you'd really do it, but as you recall, I told you to leave the boots at the bottom of the mountain.''

"But Fred said you were running out of food.''

He took his jacket off. "Do I look like I'm starving?''

"No, of course not.'' She tucked a strand of her thick straight hair behind her ear. "I don't know what I was thinking, except that it would be fun to drive a Sno-Cat. And now you're stuck with me. I'm really sorry.''

She looked up at him with liquid brown eyes and he felt a twinge of guilt for coming down so hard on her. But dammit, how was he supposed to know how to act around unexpected company, especially a woman whom he'd never expected to see in person? No wonder he'd made a mess of it. Awkwardly Max put his hand on her shoulder.

"Don't be sorry. I'm glad to have the company.'' It was true. He felt an unexpected current in the air that wasn't there before she arrived. "And I appreciate your bringing the boots.'' He felt her stiffen and he took his hand off her shoulder as casually as he could, before he offended her further by sliding his fingers across her shoulders to see if she was really wearing that long underwear under everything. "Well,'' he said brusquely, taking a package of frozen shrimp out of the bag and holding it up. "What'll it be?''

"Whatever you say. I've never had either one before.''

He raised his eyebrows in surprise. "What about blackened redfish?''

"I've heard of it. Isn't that Cajun cooking? I thought you were from Georgia.''

Startled, he turned from the freezer to look at her. "How did you know that?''

A flush crept up her cheeks and turned them bright pink. "Your accent?''

He frowned. "I thought I'd lost it.''

"You have,'' she admitted. "Fred told me.''

"Oh." He handed her a bag of frozen okra and a large cleaver. "We'll have gumbo then. Can you chop these up for me?"

She didn't answer. She just stood there for a long moment in her stockinged feet, weighing the cleaver in her hand and looking at him before she started chopping. He opened a can of tomatoes and heated olive oil in a pot. The kitchen was so small he kept brushing against her when he went to the sink or the stove. It was strange working around someone. Maybe strange wasn't the right word. It was more... distracting. He *could* tell her to take a break and he'd take over. He really didn't need her help. He didn't need anyone's help. He was completely self-sufficient. He'd been cooking by himself, living by himself and working by himself for the past year and he liked it that way.

Then he looked at her out of the corner of his eye and decided that if she were in the other room he wouldn't be able to study her profile or her long lithe legs in her stretch pants. He was trying to reconcile the picture in the catalog with the reality. It was only natural. But it wasn't necessary.

This woman was making him behave irrationally, but only because he'd been alone so long. It was the name of the game in these remote weather stations. One week on and one week off. People who lived normal lives didn't let their imaginations run wild because an unexpected guest dropped in. They didn't think about their underwear or salivate every time they got close.

He went to the cabinet for the sherry and refilled her glass. The smell of spices wafted from the pot. Feeling uncomfortable because of the silence he figured it wouldn't kill him to tell her he appreciated her effort in coming up there.

"Have I thanked you for coming all this way to bring the boots and the food?"

Steam filled the little kitchen. She tilted her face up to his. "I didn't have any choice. I promised I'd bring them and I did. Besides, I was afraid you'd complain to the management and I'd lose my job."

He nodded understandingly, but he was unaccountably disappointed. She'd thought he was some kind of crank at the same time he was thinking she was as cold as rime ice. Maybe they were both wrong. "Why don't you set the table?" He handed her some silverware and then he spooned gumbo and rice into two bowls. Before he set them on the table, he shoved an armchair to one side of the table and pulled his swivel chair to the other. She sat across from him and filled her spoon, then held it up in front of her to cool. Their eyes met and some mysterious force caused him to lift his wineglass and say, "To new boots and new friends."

She looked surprised at his toast, but she set her spoon down and silently raised her glass to his.

"And to new underwear," he added. "Is it in the box?"

She nodded and told him how much she liked the gumbo. It was true. There was a sharp kick that awakened your taste buds, then a wonderful mellow blend of shrimp and spices. "I'll bet your wife misses your cooking when you're gone," she remarked.

"I'll bet she doesn't. I don't have a wife at the moment, and I'm sure she doesn't miss anything about me." He didn't mean to sound bitter, but that was the way it came out.

"I see," she said, and he was afraid she did see, with those huge dark eyes that regarded him so solemnly. There was nothing like rehashing the past to put a damper on the present. Why did they have to talk about his ex-wife? It was time to change the subject.

He leaned back in his swivel chair and swirled the wine in his glass. "How do you like your job at Green Mountain?"

"It's all right. I like solving problems, and other people's problems are always easier to solve than your own."

"You don't look like you have any problems," he said. It was true. Her gaze was steady, her face unmarred by worry lines.

"Really? I've got a whole farm full of them, maple trees that won't produce, a sugar house that's falling apart and equipment that dates from my grandparents' time. Not that it matters. If the sap doesn't run, I won't need it."

"So you have a farm." He stirred the rice into his gumbo. "That's how you learned to drive a tractor."

She nodded. "It belonged to my grandparents, and now it's mine."

"Have you lived there all your life?" Strange how everything she said was fascinating to him, as if she'd arrived in a space ship from another planet instead of a Sno-Cat from the next state, and he wanted her to keep talking. If she did, then he wouldn't have to. He could just sit and listen and watch her lips move.

"Except for the four years I spent in New York. I used to think Northwood was the most boring place in the world. I could hardly wait to leave. So I went to seek my fortune and came home empty-handed." She smiled, but there was a sadness lurking at the back of her eyes. "I found out there are worse things than being bored."

He nodded understandingly, but he didn't understand, not really. And there was something guarded about her expression that warned him not to ask. He stood and cleared the plates from the table. "Maybe you're better at chess than seeking your fortune." He was certainly better at chess than at making casual conversation with strangers.

She tucked her legs under her in the wide comfortable chair. "I don't think so. I can't really remember much except that you're supposed to capture the king."

He placed the board on the table. "Very good. It's called checkmating."

She fingered the white ivory chess men with her long tapered fingers, setting them up on the two rows nearest her in perfect order.

"It looks like it's coming back to you," he said with a half smile. Was she the kind of player who acted dumb, then wiped up the board with her opponent? If she was, he was ready for her. "Would you like some coffee?"

Absently she lifted one of her knights off the board. "Coffee? Sure."

He stood in the doorway of the kitchen waiting for the coffee to brew, watching the light shine on her hair and turn it to gold. The smell of the coffee and the picture of her ensconced in the armchair made him think of a home and someone to come home to. Treacherous thoughts. He moved to the table with cups in his hand and cautioned himself not to get carried away. "Your move," he said.

Hesitantly she moved a pawn to King Four. He nodded approvingly. He moved his pawn to Queen Three and immediately wished he hadn't. He wasn't thinking very straight. She propped her chin in her hand and made another move. A very good move. "Who taught you to play?" he asked.

"My grandfather. He and my grandmother raised us. When his old friends died or moved away he taught me to play."

"He did a good job." He stared at the pieces. Rooks blended into pawns and pawns into knights and his mind went blank. He should be taking control of the board, but he couldn't. All he could see was her hands spread flat on the table, her unpolished nails, her only jewelry a plain gold watch with a leather band. He pulled back and surveyed the board from a different angle.

She sipped her coffee. "What about you, how did you learn?"

"I broke my leg in my senior year in high school and I had a lot of time on my hands." Too much time. Time when other guys were hanging out talking to girls with an ease he envied.

"Playing football?"

"No, skiing. So I got a book and taught myself chess. It's hard to find anyone to play with. So I play against the computer and it always wins. Are you sure you haven't played recently?"

She shook her head. "My grandfather left me the chessboard along with the farm, but I don't have any time to play." She stared off in the distance. "I told him I didn't want the farm. I had my own plans. I wonder what he'd think if he could see me now." There was a long silence.

He leaned back in his chair and studied her face, forgetting the game on the table. "He'd probably think you were doing just fine."

"Maybe," she said and the worry lines between her eyebrows disappeared. He wished they could stay that way, with the tension gone between them, until sunrise. He was so relaxed he didn't ever want to move again. But he had to move. In a few minutes he had to check the instruments.

He stood and stretched. "While you're thinking over your next move, I'm going to try my new boots."

She looked up, her eyes slightly unfocused. "In this weather?"

"This weather is what they're for. I have to take readings outside every three hours, night and day."

Her mouth fell open. "When do you sleep?"

"In three-hour segments. I'll drag a sleeping bag out and sleep on the floor. I hope my alarm won't wake you."

She got out of her chair. "I can't let you sleep on the floor because I came up here uninvited."

"Invited or not, you're a guest. Haven't you heard of Southern hospitality?"

"Haven't you heard of Yankee determination?" she countered.

For a long moment they stood staring at each other, neither one willing to back down. Finally she gave in. "Okay," she said and stretched, giving him a too-clear picture of the curve of her hips under the snug stretch pants. He tore his gaze away and ripped open the Green Mountain cardboard box and lifted the boots out. They had thick soles and a soft fleece lining.

"They look just like the picture in the catalog," he said, holding them up. But you don't, he wanted to say. Not with the clothes over the underwear and your hair framing your face as if it were silk. He bent over, pulled the boots on and tried to get a grip on himself.

"I hope they fit," she said anxiously.

"They're fine." He reached into the bottom of the box. "This must be the underwear."

Miranda scooted forward in her chair and reached for the package. For all she knew he might try it on right here and now. "You said extra large, but I think they're too big. Extra large is really large," she stammered. But he opened the bag before she could stop him and held the underwear up to his body. It wasn't hard to imagine the gray cotton knit molding to his broad shoulders and tapering to his flat stomach.

"They'll do," he said and sat down to lace his boots. She moved backward into her chair again and took a sip of wine. When he went outside she looked at her watch. So many hours before she could go home. If the weather cooperated. Restless, she got out of her chair and went to the kitchen to wash the dishes.

She was up to her elbows in soapy water when he came back, knocking the snow off the boots just outside the door. She wiped her hands on her pants and watched him remove his down vest. "What's it like out there?"

He shook his head and drops of water flew. "It's snowing." Her heart fell. When he approached, she could see the flakes in his eyebrows. "But there's a break in the altostratus clouds," he announced. Her mouth curved into a relieved smile. "You'll be glad to get out of here," he observed.

She went back to the sink. "You'll be glad to have me gone."

He found a towel and began drying the dishes she set in the wooden rack. "Not until I beat you at chess."

"That'll never happen. Not if we stay up all night."

From behind her he said, "Want to try?" in a lazy drawl that turned her knees to jelly.

She swallowed hard and handed him another plate. Their hands met and her heart stopped. His eyes weren't really blue, she realized, they were the dark blue-gray of the winter sky. "Try what, staying up all night?" Maybe it wasn't such a bad idea. It would solve the problem of who was going to sleep on the cot. And she was just competitive enough to want to win.

"It was just a suggestion."

She shrugged and dried her hands. "I'm game."

They went back to their places at the table. He checked her king, but she moved it out of the line of attack. While she waited for his next move she studied his hands, wide and strong and capable, and wondered why his wife hadn't missed him when he was gone. He had the kind of thick straight hair a woman might want to run her hands through, he was a great cook and then there was the Southern accent. He looked up and caught her staring at him and she felt the heat rise to her face.

If she wasn't careful she was going to lose her advantage. In fact she might have already lost it. She wondered when the caffeine would kick in and stimulate her defense system. She was so relaxed she felt spineless. She watched him capture her white pawn and all she could do was snuggle deeper into her chair. He gave her a cocky grin and she smiled back.

"Your casual attitude doesn't fool me," he warned. "Underneath it all there's a killer instinct." He stood. "When I come back in I'm going to show no more mercy."

She nodded and tried to focus on the board.

Outside the snow was letting up but the winds were gusting up to eighty miles per hour and visibility was around fifty feet. With the new boots he was able to walk through snowdrifts without slipping while his feet stayed completely dry. Automatically he went through his routine but his mind was back in the building. What would she do next? Check his king? Capture his knight? Disturb his hard-won tranquillity? She'd already done that. The cold air had a sobering effect on his daydreams.

He knew he couldn't have the job he wanted as a weatherman and a woman, too, so he'd chosen the job, or the job had chosen him. And his wife had chosen someone else. It was understandable. What surprised him was the way Miranda had walked into his life and filled a space he didn't know was empty. He'd dealt with loneliness before, it was always there, waiting to gain a toehold, and he'd deal with it again. Tomorrow.

He studied the sky. Tomorrow the fog would dissipate and she'd leave. But tonight there was no harm in sharing some food and wine and a game together, as long as they both knew that's all it was. She certainly did. She could hardly wait to leave. He made some notations in his log and went back inside.

Instead of making a brilliant move on the board, Miranda Morrison had fallen asleep in the deep armchair, her golden hair spread across the back of the chair like sunshine on a rainy day. He took his boots off and tiptoed across the room, his eyes never leaving her face. He took a wool blanket from the daybed and carefully draped it over her, tucking it around her feet. She stirred and he had an overwhelming desire to scoop her up into his arms. But he didn't. He knew better. He let go of the blanket and went back to his chair, swiveling back and forth, watching her sleep and thinking thoughts he usually kept in his subconscious.

The work he loved was on the front line, catching the weather where it started, just him and the elements. And that was the way he wanted it. Not for him an office downtown where they analyzed the data he sent. Down there you had people to talk to, regular hours but no excitement. No unexpected whiteouts or spectacular views of the white mountains with the moonlight on them. Up here you had to be more than a meteorologist. You had to be a welder, photographer and rescue worker. It was his kind of job and his kind of place. He didn't know why he had to remind himself of this, but he did.

When the fog disappeared at daybreak he woke her. She looked around as if she didn't know where she was. "Mount Henry, 6,000 feet," he reminded her. "You delivered a pair of boots."

She nodded and looked at the blanket he'd wrapped around her. Her gaze dropped to the chessboard on the table. "Who won?" she asked.

"Let's call it a draw." He went to the window. "Come here."

She tossed the blanket to one side and padded over to join him. It was one of those unusual days when it was possible to see all the way to the ocean, where the rising sun was reflected in the silver of the Atlantic on the horizon. "It's beautiful," she breathed. "Do you see this every day?"

He shook his head. "It's rare." Even rarer was sharing it with someone else. He was glad she liked it almost as much as he did.

She turned and sat on the daybed to put on her boots. "I appreciate your arranging the weather so I could leave today. I may even get to work on time."

He leaned against the wall and crossed his arms across his chest. "That'll be a first."

She knotted her laces and shot him a withering look. "It may not be the greatest job in the world, but I can't afford to lose it, and whether you believe it or not, I usually get there on time."

"I believe it," he said, holding her jacket out for her as she slid her arms into the sleeves. For just an instant he kept his arms on her shoulders, then he dropped them, watching as she slipped on her gloves. "What if I need to order something else?" he asked.

"There are operators on duty twenty-four hours a day."

"That's good to know."

She stood at the door, her gloved hand on the doorknob. "Thanks for everything, the food, the game, the sunrise. I'll leave the Sno-Cat just where I found it, with the keys in the ashtray. I hope Fred isn't too upset." Outside the wind and the fog had transformed the rocks and the vegetation into a fairyland of white lacy shapes. "Did you arrange this, too?" she asked.

He nodded and she got into the tractor. While he watched, she skillfully backed it up and headed down the mountain. He thought she waved before she made the first turn, but he couldn't be sure. He'd meant to tell her to drive carefully, but he didn't have a chance. She was gone.

Chapter Three

Miranda drove as fast as she dared across New Hampshire, past white fields and snow-covered farmhouses. Her eyes were heavy and her throat was dry, but she didn't dare stop for coffee. She had to get back to feed the horses and check the buckets before she went to work. Her mind was spinning with thoughts of what she'd done and how she'd keep it a secret at work. It was a crazy idea to bring the boots up there, three feet of snow or not. It was even crazier to spend the night, although she'd had no choice.

Her face burned as she relived the moment Maxwell Carter had realized she wasn't Fred. The shock on his face, and his surprise, haunted her. *Do I look like I'm starving?* he'd asked. She had to admit, she'd seen no evidence of starvation. He was the most well-built man she'd ever seen.

He couldn't believe she'd taken the Sno-Cat and driven it up by herself without asking anybody. Neither could she. What did he think of her for barging in on him that way and staying overnight? Not that he'd tried anything. Underneath his layers of winter clothing he really *was* a Southern gentleman. Or maybe he just didn't find her attractive. It didn't matter.

She left the engine of the truck running in the driveway while she emptied the hay into bins for the broad-backed horses, then squished her way to the nearest tree to check the bucket. To her surprise sap was dripping steadily into the bucket, which was already half-full. She let out a whoop of joy that startled the crows overhead. The sapping season had started. She emptied all the buckets into a twenty-gallon copper washtub and replaced them. Then with no time to change clothes, she jumped back into the truck and headed for town.

She was only ten minutes late, but her luck had run out. Old Mr. Northwood was standing at the employee entrance. "Feeling better, Miranda?" he asked dryly.

Better? What did that mean? What had her friends told him? That she'd come down with the flu? Broken her leg? Trust them to make up a good story, but what was it? "Much better," she said firmly, walking past him in her muddy boots. He followed her into the deserted lunchroom, where she filled her coffee cup while he watched.

"Have you ever thought of selling your farm?" he asked, fingering his gold watch chain. "It's such a long drive into town."

Miranda pressed her lips together. She got the message. If she lived in town she could get to work on time. "Not really," she said. "I grew up on the farm. It feels like home. And I usually enjoy the drive. It would be nice if they'd fix the potholes, though."

He nodded absently. "If you change your mind, I hope you'll come to me first. We've always wanted a little place in the country."

Miranda blinked back her surprise. She'd never call the sprawling acreage a little place in the country. Right now it was a big, unkempt, overgrown place in the mud. It had possibilities, but she thought she was the only one who could see them. It had the maple trees, it had an orchard and it had the brook running through, but they all needed a big dose of tender loving care. And that took time. Right now she needed to spend her time at Green Mountain Merchants just to pay the taxes, never mind a new engine for the tractor or tiny fir seedlings that could be the start of a Christmas tree farm on the back forty.

"I'll do that," she told Mr. Northwood, then backed out of the room and went straight to her desk. The others were all there, speaking in soothing tones to disgruntled customers, and four heads swiveled in her direction when she slid into her chair and put on her headset.

Donna finished her call and turned her attention to Miranda. "What happened?" she asked in a stage whisper. "Mr. Northwood has been breathing down our necks. Your sister is frantic and that man's called twice."

Miranda's pulse quickened. "Nothing happened. I delivered the boots. What does he want now?"

"I don't know, but you'd better call him. I promised you would. I'll call your sister and tell her you're back safe."

Miranda found Max's file and dialed his number. After only one sip of her coffee she'd developed a bad case of coffee nerves.

"Mount Henry Observation Tower."

"This is Miranda of Green Mountain Merchants. How may I help you?"

"You may help me by being there when I call. You should have been there an hour ago. I didn't know if you'd gone off the road in the Sno-Cat or..."

"I appreciate your concern. I left the Sno-Cat where I found it, and then I drove straight back here."

"What took you so long?"

She turned away from Donna's curious eyes and lowered her voice. "I went home first to check the buckets. The sap is running and I should be there right now, but I can't leave.

I was caught coming in late and there are calls waiting, so if there's nothing else . . ."

"What happened to the other boots?" he asked as if he hadn't heard a word she'd said.

"I don't know yet," she admitted, "but I'll let you know as soon as I find out. Let's say the case is closed. You have your boots and I still have my job, so far. But I really have to . . ."

"I just wanted to thank you," he said with a note of sincerity she hadn't heard before.

"You're welcome," she said and hung up.

She forced herself to concentrate on the incoming calls, not allowing herself to wonder about the weather on top of Mount Henry or the weatherman, a strange blend of rugged outdoorsman and Southern gentility. She made it until lunchtime, when they closed the complaint department for an hour and all went to eat at the steak house as they did every Friday.

They piled into Miranda's truck and peppered her with questions about the mysterious man she'd spent the night with, but she put them off until she'd driven into Chuck's parking lot and parked the truck. They squeezed into a wooden booth and all five ordered the special steak sandwich. After that there was no escaping their questions.

"Start at the beginning and tell us everything," Mavis demanded, unfolding her napkin. "What happened?"

"Nothing." Miranda's tone was so emphatic that they all laughed. She sighed. "All right. I delivered the boots to the customer because something went wrong with the mail and I got snowed in and had to spend the night. Now he has his boots, I'm home safe and we can all get back to normal."

She took a drink of water and wondered if it was normal to think so much about one customer, when there were others with problems just as serious—camera cases that wouldn't snap shut, sleeping bags with jammed zippers. But there was only one Max Carter, and even though his case was closed, she couldn't get him off her mind.

"So it was no big deal to spend the night with a customer," Donna said with a touch of disbelief. "I've never done it, have you?" She looked around the table and the others solemnly shook their heads.

"Wait a minute," Penny interjected. "Is this the guy with the Southern drawl? I wouldn't mind being stuck overnight with him. Even when he was complaining he was *sooo* charmin'...."

Miranda shook her head. "This is not the same person. Southern accent, yes, but not 'charmin',' not at all." She felt a small pang of guilt. Wasn't it charming of him to make her dinner, to offer her his bed and call just to thank her? Never mind, she wasn't under oath here; she was only trying to get off the subject. "Did I tell you the sap is running?" she asked brightly.

There was a brief pause while they all shifted gears. Lianne was the first to recover. "When's the sugaring off party?"

"This Friday," Miranda decided. "Pray for snow."

Snow wasn't all Miranda ended up praying for. She prayed for more hours in the day. Hours to process the sap that was running, no, flowing from the maple trees all day while she'd been stuck at work. The minute she got home she put on her oldest overalls over her long underwear, then a heavy plaid jacket and shoved her feet into her old rubber boots. With her hands full of pots and buckets she stumbled in the mud. She didn't even take time to hitch the horses because the sap fermented so quickly. So she hauled buckets back and forth to the sugar shack where she had a fire going. Hovering over the vats, watching the steam rise from the thin sweet sap, she felt light-headed and dizzy. When the sap had boiled down, she strained it through muslin into jars and bottles, sealed it and stored it in the root cellar where her grandmother had kept her jams and jellies.

It was close to midnight when she staggered back to the house, showered and went to bed. She knew her sister would want to talk to her, but it was too late to call, and she didn't have the energy to give her the complete account of her stay with the weatherman that she knew she'd demand. Ariel wasn't as easy to put off as her friends in Complaints. She'd want to know everything. She'd ask questions Miranda couldn't answer. How do you know he isn't married? What's he like? Does he want to see you again?

In her dreams she saw sap bubbling up over the top of the vats, running down the sides and out the door, covering the fields with sticky syrup that stuck to her boots when she walked until she couldn't move, couldn't get to work so she was late, late again. And the phones were ringing, ringing, so loudly that they woke her up. Then she realized that it was her own phone ringing, her own sister on the other end of the line, asking the questions she'd expected.

"What happened?" Ariel asked.

"Nothing," Miranda said automatically. "The sap's running. I just went to bed." She squinted at the clock on her bedside table: 7:00 a.m. "I can't talk. I have to go to work," she croaked.

"It's Saturday."

"I know it's Saturday. I have to get out and empty the buckets." She ran her hands through her tangled hair.

"I'll come out and help you and we'll talk. About you know who."

"I know who, but there's nothing to talk about."

"Oh, of course not. You made a delivery to a mysterious stranger, then you spent the night with him and you're telling me there's nothing to talk about? Give me a break."

Miranda wiggled her toes and grinned at the sarcasm in her sister's voice. "I'll give you more than a break. I'll load you down with maple syrup if you come out and help me, but if you're looking for some hot gossip you're in for a disappointment.''

"I'll be there in thirty minutes.''

Max faced his week off with mixed feelings. For the first time since he'd arrived at the observatory a little more than a year ago, he was eager to leave. He'd been restless and edgy for the past few days, exhibiting all the symptoms of cabin fever he'd thought he was immune to. When he came to Mount Henry over a year ago, he was looking for a place to escape to. The solitude, the awesome views of the white mountains and the howling winds helped him focus on the forces outside instead of the demons inside himself.

He stood at the window waiting for Jake, his replacement, to arrive, and watching it snow. The weather never let up, or if it did, it came back with a fury he couldn't ignore. His job was to observe the clouds, clock the winds and measure the snow, then phone in his observations to the Office of the Weather Bureau in Portland. They depended on him and he depended on nobody, and that's the way he liked it.

Except for the occasional stranded hiker he rescued and Fred and Jake who alternated shifts with him, he didn't see much of anyone. He didn't miss people, except for having a chess partner. That was one thing he liked about Miranda Morrison.

He couldn't figure her out. Was she a terrible player who got lucky? Or was she a good player who pretended to be terrible? And that wasn't the only puzzling thing about her. She was beautiful, but she didn't seem to know it. Even the baggy sweater couldn't hide the curves underneath, and her straight, flyaway hair only emphasized her classic features.

He'd probably never see her again. Even if he ordered from Green Mountain, it would probably get here. And if it didn't, he wouldn't call and complain, not again. He'd go there in person and make the exchange himself. It would save time and trouble. Doing business over the phone was frustrating since the invention of voice mail.

Jake finally arrived in the Sno-Cat, driven by Fred, and Max told him about the broken barometer and the crack in the altimeter before he left with the extra-large, long underwear in a paper bag. Miranda was right, extra large *was* too big. He might just drive over to Vermont and get the right size. He wasn't going to complain. It was his fault for ordering the wrong size. And if he didn't complain, he wouldn't see Miranda. So he got in his car, which was always left parked at the ranger station, and drove past snow-covered fields and white-frame farmhouses until he arrived in the small town of Northwood.

There wasn't much to it, he thought as he drove around the town square, and he wondered what kind of person would stay around and what kind of person would leave to seek a fortune elsewhere. He tried to see the place through Miranda's eyes as he drove slowly to the large redbrick building with the big green sign and parked in the lot behind the retail outlet.

The woman who waited on him gave him a startled look when he took the underwear out of the bag and for a moment he regretted bringing it back in person. After he wrote his name and address on the return form, she spent more time than he thought necessary finding the right size. Then she tried to sell him a kerosene lamp and a personalized doormat. Next she asked him if he'd ever been to a sugaring off party.

"They're a lot of fun if you've never been to one."

"I'm sure they are."

"We're having one tonight. Would you like to come?"

"That's very nice of you, but . . ."

"But you have another engagement?"

"Not really."

"Then we'll expect you at seven. Three miles south of town on Sawyer Camp Road. My sister's farm."

He stared into the woman's guileless blue eyes. "Your sister has a farm?"

She nodded. "It's not much to look at, but it's got possibilities. She's got plans for it. And she'll do what she says if I know her. She's the most determined person I know." She bit her lip. "Not too determined, though. I mean she's got it all, except for a husband. She's never been interested in any of the guys around here. I don't understand that. I married one. But enough about me. What about you, can you come to the party?"

"I don't know. There could be snow on the road."

"There'd better be snow. It's absolutely essential to have big bowls of fresh clean snow to pour the hot syrup on." She looked over his shoulder and out the window. "There it is now. Did you bring it with you from . . . where was it?"

"New Hampshire." He turned to look at the falling flakes. "No, this is Vermont snow. You can tell by the water content. Ours is drier."

The woman grinned delightedly, as if he'd said something witty. "See you tonight."

Max smiled noncommittally and walked out into the falling snow. He had no intention of going to a party where he knew no one with the possible exception of Miranda Morrison. Of course it might not be her farm or her party or her sister. There must be many women with farms and sisters in Vermont, and they probably all threw parties to celebrate the season. He'd never been to a sugaring off party, but he'd been to other parties, enough of them to know he didn't want to go to any more of them.

At parties there were people making small talk. A lot of noise, a lot of smoke and loud music. But he didn't really want to go home, either, so he walked down Main Street with his hands in his pockets, the snow melting as it hit his head of thick blond hair. He stopped at a diner and sat in a vinyl booth and ordered a piece of apple pie. The waitress called him honey, and he wondered where this rumor about

New Englanders being cool and standoffish had gotten started.

As he ate he also wondered what people did at a sugaring off party besides eat snow with syrup. Not that he was thinking of going, but it would be interesting to find out. What would Miranda think if he showed up tonight? For all he knew she hadn't enjoyed her unexpected overnight with him and didn't want any further contact.

No, there was no reason to go to her party. The sister was just being friendly, like the waitress. They called you honey or invited you to parties, but they didn't expect you to respond. On the other hand, he had nothing else to do. He didn't mind driving in the snow with his four-wheel drive. And he wouldn't mind seeing Miranda again. If it was her farm, that is. Determined, her sister had said. Yes, that sounded like her. He ordered a cup of coffee, picked up the local newspaper and settled down to wait until 7:00.

Miranda let the back door slam behind her and headed for the sugar shack, her arms full of plates and cups, her shoes crunching through the snow. There were people in the living room, people in the kitchen and more people arriving by the minute at the front door. But it was in the sugar shack, that small wooden frame shed behind the house, where the main attraction would take place. From within a cloud of steam her sister was stirring the syrup in two pots at the same time.

"How's it coming?"

Ariel looked up and smiled. "Coming along, coming along. What time is it anyway?"

Miranda glanced at her watch. "Seven-thirty. Why? There's no hurry. Everyone's having a good time judging by the noise level."

Ariel wiped her hands on her apron. "Who all's arrived?" she asked, studying her sister's face carefully.

"The Ashtons with children, the Bensons without Hank, Jerry, Linda, Marcia. Go on in and say hello. I'll watch the syrup."

"No," Ariel insisted. "It's your party. You're the hostess. You ought to be there to greet everybody."

"The front door's unlocked. Everybody knows everybody. They don't need me."

"No, they don't. I mean, yes, they do." Ariel gave her sister a playful shove. "Now go on back."

"Turn the fire down and we'll both go back. It's your party as much as mine. You invited half the people."

Ariel's forehead wrinkled under a fringe of feathered bangs. "I just wish I knew if they're all coming." They turned the burners to low, then ran back to the house through the still falling snow.

Above the voices Miranda heard the front doorbell ring. Weaving her way through friends and neighbors and stepping on an occasional toe, she shouted, "Come in," but the ringing continued. Was she the only one who heard it? The couple nearest the door were so engrossed in each other they didn't even look up. "Excuse me," she said, brushing past them. Who would ring the bell, anyway, seeing all the cars, hearing the noise and seeing the lights?

She opened the door and a gust of cold wind hit her in the face and sucked the air from her lungs. She gasped. She stumbled backward. The man standing in the doorway looked like Max Carter. Had the same broad shoulders that filled the door frame, the same thick blond hair blown across his forehead, the same blue eyes that gazed down at her intently. It had to be him, but it *couldn't* be him. What would he be doing at her house on a Friday night? She wished she could ask him, but she was completely out of breath, and her lips were too numb to form the words.

Other people didn't seem to have any problem moving their lips. "Come in and close the door," they shouted.

Miranda shrugged her shoulders helplessly and reached for the doorknob. Max Carter came in and she closed the door.

"You weren't expecting me?" he asked, noting her reaction.

She shook her head.

"I shouldn't have come."

She opened her mouth and the words tumbled out at last. "Of course you should. But how . . . where . . . ?"

"Your sister invited me." He crossed his arms over his chest. "I thought you knew."

She shook her head. "It doesn't matter. She invited a lot of people."

His eyes left hers for a moment and scanned the crowd. "So I see."

Miranda leaned against the carved newel post at the foot of the staircase nearby, hoping he wouldn't notice that her knees were too weak to hold her up without support. She felt so shaky, so breathless, but that was just because she was so surprised to see him. That was all.

There was a long silence while his gaze returned to hers, his blue eyes making a leisurely tour of her long loose hair, her eyes, her mouth and then the contours of her striped polo shirt.

She turned toward the kitchen, desperate for some fresh air and some space away from the heated gaze of her unexpected guest, but bumped into Mavis and Lianne, who were bearing down on her, their eyes on Max.

"Who's your friend?" Mavis hissed. "Don't you dare leave this room until you've introduced us."

"Of course." Miranda turned and almost crashed into Max, who was right behind her. "Uh, Maxwell Carter, meet my friends, Lianne and Mavis. And now if you'll excuse me I'll go check on the syrup."

Lianne gripped her arm tightly. "We just checked. It's not quite ready." Her gaze shifted to Max. "Are you the man, you *can't* be the man with the boots, can you?"

"Ah certainly can," he drawled and proceeded to explain the whole story to them. It might have been her imagination, but to Miranda his accent seemed a little stronger tonight, a little more appealing than she'd remembered. And she could tell by the rapt expressions on the faces of her friends that they thought so, too.

When Max paused in his narrative, the two women looked at each other and sighed. "We didn't know you'd be here tonight."

Max smiled. "Neither did I."

"Ariel invited him," Miranda explained.

"Ohh," they exclaimed. "There she is now."

Ariel was gliding toward them as if there was no crowd, just as she used to do in high school when the place was full of her friends. She was always in command of any social situation, always trying to arrange dates for her younger sister, convinced that Miranda, though beautiful, had no feminine wiles to rely on. But this time she'd gone too far. She could have at least warned her, so she could have been prepared instead of acting like a shell-shocked victim at the front door. Miranda still hadn't completely recovered from the shock, but she'd recovered enough to speak to Ariel. And she couldn't wait until she got her alone.

"What a surprise to see Max," she said, giving her sister a pointed glance.

Ariel turned on her warmest smile. "Is that his name?" She held out her hand. "I'm happy to meet you."

"And now if you'll excuse us," Miranda interrupted, taking Ariel firmly by the elbow. "We've got to check on something."

"Oh, I don't..." Ariel couldn't refuse without making a scene, and Miranda made the most of it by hustling her back out in the snow behind the house.

"How could you?" Miranda sputtered the moment they were alone, snowflakes falling on her head.

"How could I what? I swear to you on Grandpa's bible, I didn't know who he was. He comes in to the store at five o'clock tonight and says he's never been to a sugaring off party. What was I supposed to do, ignore him?"

"Nothing, absolutely nothing. I should have known you were up to something. I'm surprised you didn't invite the whole store full of customers."

Ariel chewed her lip thoughtfully as if she wished she had.

"What was he doing in the store?"

"Exchanging his long underwear."

"And I suppose you didn't recognize it?"

"Of course not. I sell a ton of long underwear. And even if I did recognize the underwear and the Southern accent, what's wrong with inviting him to our party? You told me yourself he wasn't an ax murderer."

Miranda sighed. "Did it occur to you that if I'd wanted to invite him to the party, I would have?"

Ariel shivered in the cold air. "Could we continue this discussion later? I'm freezing." With that she plowed through the swiftly falling snow to the sugar shack, Miranda at her heels. Without speaking, they each took a long wooden spoon and stirred the thickening syrup. Miranda took several deep steadying breaths before her heart slowed to a normal rate and her knees stopped shaking.

"You have to admit he's very attractive," Ariel said with a sidelong glance at her sister.

"I admit it, he's very attractive," she conceded.

"And he's definitely interested in you."

"How do you know that?"

"I saw how he looked at you."

"I saw how he looked at me, too, just like he looks at everyone else. He works on top of this mountain, as I told you, without any people around. So when he's around people, he looks at them more intently than other people do, that's all. So don't go making something out of nothing. I have no room in my life for men, and no time, either. And neither does he. You should see how he lives, completely self-sufficient and independent.''

"Yes, you told me. But you didn't tell me he was gorgeous and to-die-for. And *I'm* telling *you* that if you don't get back in there Mavis and Lianne, and half the other unmarried women in town, are going to be all over him.''

Miranda widened her gaze in mock horror. "Oh, no. You mean I'll lose the last eligible man to ever cross my threshold? What do you suggest, that I invite him out here to watch the syrup harden?''

Ariel nodded enthusiastically. "Now you're catching on.''

"If I'm catching on, don't you think he'll catch on, too?''

Miranda's words hung in the air even as Ariel looked up from the pot, her gaze fastened on the door of the sugar shack and on the man who'd appeared in the doorway. "Mr. Carter," she gushed, "you're just in time to watch the syrup harden. If you'll excuse me . . .'' And before Miranda could protest, her traitorous sister had disappeared through the open door and slammed it shut behind her.

Automatically Miranda gripped the handle of the spoon and dragged it through the thickening sap.

"Can I help?'' Max asked.

"Uh, sure. You can pour the syrup into these jars.'' Might as well keep him busy, then they wouldn't have to talk. She wouldn't have to explain her overeager sister, her run-down farm or her own peculiar behavior.

Max filled the jars, set the pot down and leaned against the wall to watch Miranda as she tasted the syrup thickening into maple sugar. Her eyes closed in concentration, she licked her lips, leaving a film of sugar coating them. A shaft of desire shot through him. He wanted to taste her lips, to test her response. He'd wanted it from the first moment he'd seen her at his weather station, when she'd been windblown and wide-eyed. He'd resisted then, but now, alone in this steam-filled shack, with the snow falling silently outside, he didn't know how much longer he could hold out.

She looked up and caught her breath at the look in his eyes. "Would you like a taste?" she asked, then instantly regretted it.

She held out the wooden spoon and he took it from her and laid it on the counter. Did he want a taste? He'd never wanted anything so much in his life. He tilted her chin with his knuckles and kissed her firmly on her sugarcoated mouth. Her hands moved to his shoulders to push him away, but never quite got around to it. Instead she closed her eyes and leaned into the kiss.

It was minutes or maybe hours when he realized they were stuck together. It was only by licking her lips and his, tongues entwined as she tried to help that they finally pulled apart. Her eyes were soft brown velvet, her face flushed either from the steam or the kiss. She was the most desirable woman he'd ever seen and one taste was not enough. He wanted more and he thought she did, too.

"I'm afraid you have the wrong idea about me," she said, stepping back from the stove as if the heat was too much for her. "I'm really not looking for this kind of thing. When I asked you if you wanted a taste, it was just to see, to get your professional opinion."

"Of the syrup."

"Of course."

He shrugged. "I really can't tell. I'm afraid I'm going to have to have some more."

She folded her arms across her chest and regarded him with mock outrage. Reluctantly her lips curved upward and a small giggle escaped from her throat.

His mouth stretched into a broad grin and he knew why he'd come to this party. For just this, this one moment in this small shack, with this woman smiling at him and him grinning back, a perfect moment frozen in time.

The magic lasted only a moment, until the pounding on the door of the shack and the voices demanding to know when the syrup would be ready shattered it. The door burst open and they poured in, the men in their flannel shirts, the women in Shetland sweaters and wool stretch pants. Max left the shack to make room for them and walked slowly through the cold night air, not feeling the chill or seeing the snow that fell faster and harder. He walked around to the front of the house, still in a daze, still tasting Miranda and the sugar on her lips.

He couldn't see his car, parked somewhere at the end of the driveway, but he knew it was there and he knew he ought to find it and get out of there while he still had some remnants of self-control left. How often did he have to remind himself that such women as Miranda Morrison were off limits to him? What he should do was get into his car and drive as fast and as far away from her as he could and never come back. Never order anything from Green Mountain Merchants again. There were other mail-order companies, other complaint departments who were not manned by beautiful goddesses in form-fitting underwear. If he needed winter gear he could order it from them.

She'd understand if he left now. She probably wouldn't even miss him with all those other people in there clamoring for her attention. He circled the house for the second time, unwilling to break his solitude by joining the merriment. He reminded himself he'd only seen her twice in his life. Then why did he feel he'd known her forever?

As he passed the back door, a snowball whizzed past his ear and he ducked and looked around. Smothered laughter came from behind a maple tree. He discovered a small boy with his hand poised to throw another snowball.

"Hey," Max protested. "Pick on somebody your own size."

The boy laughed aloud. "Sorry. I wasn't aiming at you. I was trying to get my brother back." A snowball hit Max in the back. "See, that's him. Help me get him."

Obligingly Max bent over and made a snowball with his bare hands and aimed it at the outline of the older, larger boy across the yard but missed. Both boys came out in the open then, firing at each other, then at Max, getting closer with every round of white frozen missiles. They hurled insults at each other along with the snowballs. Max joined in, chuckling to himself at their colorful language, regretting having been an only child and growing up in the South where there was no snow and no snowball fights. He made another snowball, packed it hard and launched it into the darkness just for fun. But at that moment Miranda came out of the shack and it hit her on the shoulder.

"Scott, Brian?" she called. "Where are you? I sent you out for fresh snow, and you're having a snowball fight."

"We didn't do it, Aunt Miranda," they chorused. "*He* did."

"Who?" she asked, peering into the darkness.

"Me," Max answered. "Are you okay?"

"You got snow down my neck," she remarked, and in an instant she bent over, formed a snowball and hit him square in the chest. The boys dropped the snow in their hands to watch, fascinated, while the adults acted more childish than they did.

Max stepped behind a maple tree and took advantage of the darkness to sneak up behind Miranda and grab her by the shoulders. She squirmed out of his grasp and ran into the field. Max chased her while the boys whooped and cheered them on.

Miranda stumbled on a dead limb and fell headfirst into a soft snowdrift. Max threw himself down beside her and pulled her up to face him. "You don't fight fair," she said breathlessly.

"That's because I don't know the rules," he answered. "We don't have this white stuff in Georgia." Breathing hard, he brushed the snow off her face with his fingers, wishing he could kiss it off her eyebrows, eyelids and lips. There was a long silence while she looked at him expectantly, but he wasn't sure what she expected from him. He helped her to her feet. "How's the party going?" he asked.

"Fine. I have to get back. Some people are leaving. Do you want some coffee or anything?"

He shook his head and walked her back to the house. "Later. I'm still learning some techniques from your nephews."

"Be careful. They're ruthless, and their language would make a sailor blush."

"I'll keep my ears covered," he promised and watched her walk up the steps to the kitchen.

Miranda stood at the front door, saying good-night to the Bensons, the Ashtons, Hank, Jerry, Linda, Marcia and dozens of others. It was like old times but different. She was an adult now, responsible for the farm and keeping it intact for future generations of Morrisons, should there be any. It was a scary thought with the farm in disrepair and no future Morrisons in sight except for her nephews, who might or might not be interested in working worn-out acreage when they grew up.

Their father, her brother-in-law, probably had other plans for them. With these thoughts tumbling around in her brain, she smiled and thanked everyone for coming. She hadn't seen Max for half an hour and she wondered if he'd gone without saying goodbye.

She was still in a state of shock from his appearance at the party. And then there was the kiss. The kiss that had shaken her more than she cared to admit. She wondered why he hadn't kissed her again in the field.

Before she left, Lianne hugged Miranda. "It was a wonderful party, just like old times, only better. And Max is adorable. I can't believe you holding out on us like that."

"I didn't, I swear...."

"It's so cute the way he's buttering up your nephews out there in the snow. Oh, there he is now. See you Monday unless you're too tired to come in if you know what I mean." Then she was gone and so was everybody else except for Ariel, her husband and her boys, who were in their jackets teaching Max some karate moves in the living room. Ariel stood on the front porch calling her men. Then she looked up at the sky as the snowflakes fell into her open mouth.

"I may not be a weatherman," she said loudly, "but I know when a storm is coming and I wouldn't advise anyone to drive any distance tonight." The boys finally jumped off the front porch and Ariel took her husband's arm to keep from slipping on the front walk. They called their goodbyes and there was silence at last.

Miranda closed the heavy oak front door and leaned back against it. The coals glowed from the fire she'd built hours ago in the brick fireplace. There were dirty glasses and empty bowls scattered everywhere and all she wanted to do was go upstairs and soak in a hot tub, then fall into her feather bed. But outside in the snow, the sap continued to drip into the buckets and had to be collected before it overflowed. And inside she felt the tension between Max and her heat up the atmosphere, the memory of their kiss hanging in the air. It was time to leave, but he showed no signs of leaving. What should she do, what should she say?

He was gazing absently into the dying coals, his arm on the mantel above the fireplace, his dark blond hair slanted across his forehead. She pressed her palms together and moved restlessly toward the staircase. "It might be dangerous to drive to New Hampshire tonight," she suggested.

"I think I can make it."

Was this the moment for her to repay his hospitality by offering him a place to spend the night? No, it was not. It was the time to say good-night, politely but firmly. But before the message could get to her brain she heard herself say, "You're welcome to stay here." Her eyes strayed to the lumpy old couch and she knew she ought to warn him it would be the most uncomfortable night of his life, but she didn't. She held her breath.

"OK," he said.

"OK," she echoed and reached into the hall closet for the extra blankets and pillow on the top shelf. Telling herself this was no big deal, she set them on the end of the couch. Many people had spent the night on that old couch. He was not the first to take refuge from the weather and he wouldn't be the last. So there was no reason for her pulse to race, for her mind to flood with images of his long lean body trying to adapt to the lumps on the couch. She took her jacket off the coatrack and thrust her arms into the sleeves. "Make yourself comfortable." If you can, she thought guiltily.

"Where are you going?"

"Out to empty the buckets. When the sap runs, it really runs. And it won't last, maybe a few more weeks is all. So I have to take advantage of it."

"Can I help?"

She looked at his feet. "Did you bring your boots?"

"No, but I've got my long underwear on."

She didn't dare meet his gaze. That underwear again, stretched across his broad shoulders and solid muscles. "I've got extra rubber boots," she said, "if you're sure you're up for this."

"Let's go."

Chapter Four

The temperature was falling quickly, just as it should during sapping season, and an almost full moon had risen and shone on the freshly fallen snow. Miranda pulled an old wooden sled behind her with empty plastic gallon milk containers on it across the field toward the grove of maples. She'd been coming out alone every night that week and it felt strange to have someone with her. A shiver of anticipation went up her spine. Or was it just the cold night air?

"Normally I'd hitch up the horses, but it's too late," she explained.

"For them or for you?" he inquired.

"Both of us. They're old and tired, but I love them. And I couldn't do without them. Tomorrow we'll bring them out, you'll see—" She broke off. Had she really said, "Tomorrow *you'll* see?" Tomorrow he'd be gone. She hoped he hadn't noticed her slip of the tongue.

At the first maple he unhooked the full plastic bucket before she could, set it on the sled and replaced it with an empty one. All with seeming effortlessness, as if he'd lived on a maple sugar farm all his life. They moved on to the next tree, but this time she made the first move. After all, this was her farm and it *was* her job.

"This is amazing. You put a hole in a tree and out comes pure maple syrup," he said, watching her.

"Not quite. First you have to choose the southern exposure that yields the most sap. And it takes forty gallons of sap to make one gallon of syrup."

"Is that what you were doing in the shack, turning sap into syrup?"

"Yes, while you were out throwing snowballs at my nephews."

"Those kids are ruthless. I had to defend myself. Good thing you came out and rescued me." He took one of the ropes out of her hands and together they pulled the full sled across the snow toward the shack.

"Sorry I couldn't rescue you from my sister."

"Your sister?" He slanted a glance in her direction. "I take it she wasn't supposed to invite me here tonight."

"No, that's not it." Miranda jerked her end of the rope. "She can invite whoever she wants ... but I'll bet she didn't give you a chance to say no. When she puts her mind to something, she never quits."

"That's funny. That's what she said about you, that you were very determined. It must run in the family."

Miranda smiled and pulled the door to the shack open. "You could say that." The twenty-gallon galvanized washtub was already on the stove, so they filled it with the sap, bucket by bucket, waiting and watching for it to come to a boil in silence. "I love her dearly," Miranda said at last, "but ..."

"But you don't want her meddling in your life. Especially your love life."

"I don't have a love life," She leaned over the tub so he wouldn't see the flush that rose to the top of her head.

"That's the problem. *Her* problem, not mine," she corrected quickly.

"Of course," he agreed. "Anyone can see you're the independent type."

"Thank you." She looked up and gave him a sharp glance. Wasn't that the same word she'd used to describe him to Ariel?

"She looks happy. Maybe she just wants to see you married so you can be as happy as she is."

Miranda gripped the lid on the evaporator. "That's exactly what she wants. How did you know?"

"Just a lucky guess."

"The point is—" she set the lid down with a clatter "—that, among other things, I came back from New York to get away from men, or a certain type of man that I saw too much of there, and so far I've succeeded nicely. Now if I could only be as successful at making this farm pay its way..."

"Everything would be perfect."

She nodded vigorously. Strange how she'd never realized that blue eyes could be just as warm and understanding as brown, maybe more.

"What happened in New York?" he asked, leaning back against the rough-edged wooden table.

She sighed. "What *didn't* happen? I was mugged, harassed and burglarized."

"So you came back to Northwood."

"Yes, and I've never regretted it. It's just..." She closed her eyes for a moment. "Sometimes I get so tired." Before she could open her eyes she felt his arms around her, holding her steady, offering comfort, understanding and maybe more. For a brief moment she wanted to let herself go, give in to the fatigue and longing and let him hold her and see where it would lead to. But the truth hit her like a wet snowball. He feels sorry for you, she told herself, especially after hearing your sad story. And pity is the last thing you want or need.

She raised her head and gave him a shaky smile. "I don't know what's wrong with me. I don't usually go to pieces like this. It must be late and I'm losing it." Pulling away from him, she reached for the valve and shut the gas burners off. "We'll let it freeze overnight, then we... *I* can just lift off the ice in the morning and the syrup will be underneath. Simple, yes?"

He put his arm across her shoulder. "Yes," he said and wished he could capture the feeling again, of holding her in his arms, aware of the lush curves of her breasts under her shirt. But she ducked under his arm and led the way out of the shack and back to the house. They walked single file, boots crunching through the snow in harmony, but without speaking or touching. Her choice, not his.

His choice would have been to go arm in arm, hip against hip, thigh against thigh. Maybe he shouldn't have come tonight. They were not only back to zero, but they had also regressed a few points below. Because of what, the kiss, the sister, her fatigue? Did she regret inviting him to spend the night? Should he offer to leave?

He closed the living-room door behind them. She put a log on the hot coals. The pungent smell of the hickory smoke and the welcome heat from the fire made his decision for him. He'd stay till dawn, and then leave before she woke up, leaving a note on the table. "Sorry to have inconvenienced you," it would say. "Best of luck, Max."

She paused on the bottom step of the varnished staircase. "Thanks for your help."

"My pleasure. I mean it. I enjoyed it. I've never been on a farm before."

She ran her fingers around the carved newel post. "Never?"

"Nope. I've been on mountaintops studying weather patterns for the past years. Before that I lived in Atlanta."

''Where you broke your leg skiing.''

His gaze met hers. ''You remembered.'' She looked embarrassed to be caught doing so. ''Actually I broke it in North Carolina skiing. We don't have any mountains in Georgia.''

Like a rag doll she sank down to sit on the second step, wrapping her arms around her knees. ''What is it about mountains anyway?''

He sat on the couch, feeling the springs bounce back against his thighs. He stared out the small windowpanes and into the moonlit snowscape, thinking. He knew what it was, but he didn't know how to put it into words, and it seemed important to explain it to her. ''It's partly the isolation, the feeling that you're all alone in the world, above the mess and the muck of cities and the people who live there. But it's more than that.''

''It's the confrontation with the elements,'' she suggested.

''How do you know that?''

''I was there, remember?''

His gaze swiveled toward hers and locked. ''I remember. I don't get that many guests.'' He remembered everything about that evening. The way she'd looked sleeping in his chair, wrapped in his blanket. . . .

''Welcome or unwelcome.''

''You were welcome,'' he assured her.

''You made me feel that way. With the drinks and the dinner. And I haven't offered you anything. Not even a glass of Grandma's mulberry wine.'' She stood and went to the cabinet in the corner, took out a cut-glass decanter and two small matching glasses. Noting the bemused look on his face, she smiled and handed him a glass of the dark red wine. ''You didn't think farmers lived like savages, did you?''

He sniffed the wine appreciatively. ''I didn't think about farmers at all until, when was it, two weeks ago?'' He leaned back on the couch and crossed his leg over his knee, watching her take her place back on the hard varnished chair step again, her blond hair falling forward against her pale cheek. He put the palm of his hand on the cushion next to him. "Wouldn't you be more comfortable here?"

She smiled. "Knowing that old couch, I doubt it. Besides, I'm on my way up to bed." As if to prove it, she stood up again, one hand on the railing, the other wrapped around her wineglass.

He wished he could think of something to say, something to keep her there talking, sipping wine and listening to the wood hiss as the sap oozed out of it. But he had never been much good at making small talk.

"I was surprised you came tonight. I didn't know you liked parties."

"I don't usually. But I thought this would be an interesting cultural experience."

Reflected light from the fire danced in her dark eyes. "I hope you weren't disappointed."

He stretched his long legs and stood, then moved deliberately toward her. He put his hand over hers on the banister and looked down at her. "I learned a lot. More than I expected."

He cupped her chin with his hand and she stared up into his eyes, now pools of dark blue. She swallowed hard and tried to look away but couldn't. If she didn't do something soon she'd be back in his arms again, his strength making her feel warm and protected. And if he kissed her she just might, because it was late and she was feeling the effects of the wine, she just might kiss him back.

"There's something I have to explain to you, Max," she said, unable to hide the slight tremor in her voice.

He traced his thumb up the side of her cheek to her temple. "Yes?" he asked, his slow drawl stretching the word out into extra syllables.

She took a deep breath. "It's nothing personal, but I'm really not interested in men at this time." There, she'd said it.

"Really?" His mouth was so close she could feel his warm breath against her lips. If he got any closer he'd make a liar out of her and she couldn't have that happen, she just couldn't. She had her future to think about and the future of this farm. Right now she should be in bed resting up for a full day's work tomorrow and instead she was drinking and flirting with danger in the form of a tall, handsome weatherman.

"Yes, really," she said, backing her way up the steps. "But someday when I've got the farm in order and I make a go of it on my own, well then maybe..."

"You could give me a call."

She took another backward step up and away from him. "Yes, sure." There, what was so hard about that? He understood. She stood looking down at him, trying to read the expression in his eyes.

"I'll be looking forward to it," he said with a gleam in his eye.

She hurried up the remaining stairs. Deep in the depths of her feather bed, she pondered his easy acceptance of her refusal. Maybe he was relieved to know she wasn't available. Anyway, she felt sure he'd be gone before her alarm went off. She tried to fall asleep, knowing she had work to do the next day, but the images kept running through her mind. His face by firelight, the smell of the wood smoke and the touch of his hand on hers. The feel of fresh snow on her face and the taste of his kiss on her lips. Why couldn't she put him out of her mind? Why did all thoughts of the party center around Max? Was it because he was the only guest who was still there? She felt like a love-starved teenager, tossing in her old bed under the eaves.

She stared at the window at the frost forming around the edges of the panes. She wasn't a teenager, but she must be starved for love. It was the only explanation for this restless yearning she felt. Starved for love or just hungry, it didn't matter. She was going to have to get along without love for a while. For a *long* while. Until the farm was paying for itself. Until she could quit her job and devote full-time to it. Until she was self-sufficient and independent. Then she could think about love.

Until then she had to think maple syrup. Maybe if she counted jars and bottles... Finally she fell into a deep sleep until her alarm went off the next morning. The smell of coffee wafted up the stairway. She tossed her brushed cotton nightgown aside and pulled on a fresh pair of thermal knit underwear, layered a turtleneck polo shirt and plaid flannel pants over it. All of it purchased with her discount from Green Mountain Merchants. She thrust her feet into her fully lined moosehide slippers and tiptoed downstairs. The couch was back to normal, or as normal as a thirty-five-year-old couch could be, no sign of the blanket Max had used, no sign of him. She peered out the front window. His car was still there.

And so was he. Standing in the kitchen, leaning against the counter, his hair rumpled, his face unshaven, as if he belonged there.

"Coffee?" he asked, furthering the illusion that he was the host and she was the guest.

She held out her hand and accepted the full cup. "Thank you."

He turned toward the stove. "I'm making pancakes. Got any syrup?"

She smiled. "I think so." Opening the refrigerator, she took out a jar of dark thick syrup from her first batch, along with a block of unsalted butter. Then she stood back and watched him pour batter into a cast-iron skillet and the childhood memories came flooding back.

"My grandfather used to make breakfast on the weekends," she said. "He said Grandma deserved a rest."

He flipped a pancake. "Nice man."

"Very nice. He hadn't counted on another family to raise when he got us dumped on his doorstep."

Max looked at her over his shoulder. "What happened to your parents?"

"They were killed in a car crash on the tollway just south of Brattleboro. We were staying here on the farm while they went to an auction. We never left. I was only two, I don't really remember them. But Ariel does."

Max handed her a plate with a large fluffy pancake on it and she sat down at the kitchen table. "I think she's always felt she had to be both my mother and my sister. Especially after the folks died."

"And that's why she won't rest until she gets you settled down." He took the seat opposite her at the round oak table.

"Could be."

They ate in silence while he thought about two little girls and their grandfather tossing pancakes in this same kitchen, in that same pan. "I envy you the sense of belonging you must feel, living here, knowing you'll always live here."

"I don't know that. Grandpa used to have four hundred acres. He had to sell off over the years, until now we've only got eighty. If I can't make it pay..." She trailed off, unwilling to think of the alternatives. A few minutes later, she set her fork down and slid her chair back from the table. "And if I don't get busy I won't ever make it pay. Thanks for the breakfast and for the help last night. I see the skies are clearing..."

"And the temperature's rising," he interrupted, clearing the table. "Perfect weather for sapping, wouldn't you say?"

"Yes, but you've done your part. I'm sure you're anxious to get going, to salvage something of the weekend before it's over and you have to go back to work."

"I don't go back to work this week. Since we work twenty-four hours a day, we're off one week and on the next.

This is my week off." He didn't see how she could refuse his help, but he could see her mind spinning, thinking of reasons. It was his job to get her moving and stop thinking.... What had happened to his determination to leave before she awoke? Gone, disappeared, forgotten. He only knew that when he'd gotten up that morning he'd had an overwhelming desire to make breakfast for her in that old-fashioned kitchen and spend the day doing what she did. "Let's go," he said, walking into the living room to take her jacket off the coatrack.

She held out her arms obediently, but there were tiny worry lines etched between her eyebrows. What was she afraid of? That he'd overstay his welcome? That he'd compromise her independence? He valued his own independence too much to ever do that. Still, he realized he'd have to tread lightly. Without talking, they pulled on their rubber boots—which were standing next to each other by the front door where they'd left them last night—and their gloves, which were still on the mantel where they'd been left to dry.

The snow was turning to slush under their feet and the air felt almost muggy as the temperature edged its way toward forty degrees Fahrenheit. It was easier by daylight to see what they were doing, skimming the ice off the syrup in the shack and using the broad-back workhorses to carry the full buckets. They snorted steam from their huge nostrils as Miranda led them out of the barn.

"Meet Hans and Gretel," Miranda said, fastening the worn leather harnesses onto their backs. "They're Ariel's really. She named them. She used to pretend they were racehorses and she was the first female jockey in Vermont."

Max reached up to scratch the horses between the ears. At the first tree Miranda put a lid on the full plastic bucket and hooked it to the harness. "It's a lot easier than using the sled," she explained as they moved on to the next tree. "But by now I'd hoped to have a pipeline from the trees to the shack.''

"How would the horses get their exercise?" he asked, tightening the leather straps.

"Ariel still rides them, and her kids do, too, when they come out. But after all these years they're ready to retire to the back pasture." She gestured toward the land beyond the trees. "The horses, not the kids."

"Maybe they like feeling useful," he suggested, looking up into the horse's huge brown eyes behind a shaggy fringe of hair.

"Do you know anything about farm animals?" she asked, an amused tone in her voice.

"No, but I know something about being useful. Why don't I take Hans, or is it Gretel, and get the trees over there?"

Replacing an empty bucket on the nail, Miranda nodded. He couldn't see her face but he hoped she was glad to have him there, if only to have an extra pair of hands, another warm body to make the work go faster. He had no idea how she felt about him. For the moment he would just have to take her at her word. That she was too busy working on the farm to think about men. That she was here to get away from a certain type of man. Was he the type she was running from? He hoped not. Because she was the type he'd been looking for all his life.

The type who followed her dream, who didn't give up when things went wrong. Who knew enough to come home to her farm when she found the city wasn't the place for her. And who worked that farm with every ounce of determination she had. He knew she'd fight for what she wanted, he only wished she wanted him as much as he wanted her.

He heaved the full bucket and attached it to the horse's harness. How ironic. He'd found the woman he'd been looking for just after realizing he couldn't have any woman at all, no matter what type, and also have the job he loved.

How many times did he have to remind himself that there wasn't a woman alive worth giving up his work for? He grabbed the bridle and he and the horse trudged ankle deep in mud toward the sugar shack.

But spending one weekend on a maple sugar farm with a beautiful woman was far from giving up his job. Hadn't he decided to get out and meet people? Well, that's what he was doing. Spending a weekend in the country. The note he'd planned to leave on the table was long forgotten. He was planning on the whole weekend and he hoped she was, too. She must know there was too much work for one person here.

On the other hand she might be too idealistic, too impractical to realize the obvious. She wanted to quit her job and make the farm pay for itself, but even if she made syrup year-round instead of for a few weeks, she couldn't make enough. He didn't know much about farming, but he knew farmers had to diversify. Like serving chicken dinners on Sundays and selling blackberries from a roadside stand. But that wasn't his problem. It was hers. It was her farm and her syrup and he was a guest, and he'd keep his opinions to himself.

They worked all morning, then took a short break for lunch—vegetable soup from a can. In the afternoon they split up. Miranda stayed in the shack, keeping the fire going under the galvanized washtub. When the syrup was thick and still hot, she strained it through sheets of muslin into jars, and sealed them. Max kept her supplied with sap, hauling it by horseback from the farthest trees along the creek until every bucket on the place was empty again. For a few hours, anyway.

He took the horses to the barn and went back to the shack. She'd lined some of the jars along the windowsill and was admiring the pale amber syrup when he walked in. "Look at this color," she said. "The lighter the syrup, the more delicate the taste."

"In the South we bake beans with maple syrup," he said, his gaze shifting from the amber syrup to her hair, the fading sunlight turning it to burnished gold.

She turned to face him, and he had to grip the edge of the table to steady himself. All afternoon he'd thought about getting the sap into buckets and the buckets into the shack. And now suddenly all he could think about was Miranda... and how he could get her into his arms.

"Sounds good," she said, suddenly looking so tired he thought she might collapse. "What kind of beans do you use?" she asked, twisting the lid on a quart jar.

"Yellow eyes or baby limas," he said, while his eyes swept over her soft clinging cotton shirt and the long lines of her flannel pants.

"I've got some red kidney beans."

"Fine."

She moved toward the door, a half smile tugging at the corner of her mouth. "You're easy," she remarked.

He took her arm as she passed and pulled her toward him. Her huge dark eyes were startled like a fawn's, but then melted as he bent to kiss her. He felt her arms go around his neck and he felt his heart pound. Maybe he was wrong. Maybe he was her type after all.

There was no sugar on her lips to hold them together this time, but they didn't need it; all they needed was mutual desire, a desire that he felt throbbing deep inside himself as her lips parted and her tongue met his. But it didn't last. He should have known it was too good to last. Gasping for breath, she pulled away.

"Max," she said. "I can't do this, not with you, not with anybody. I'm grateful to you, but..."

"But not that grateful."

"Yes. No. It's not that." Tears of frustration formed and glazed her dark eyes.

He brushed her cheek with his thumb. "You don't have to explain. I'm sorry. I took advantage of you, of your hospitality. And your need . . . for my help," he added.

Shakily she raised her head and met his gaze. "It's my fault. I shouldn't have . . ." She shook her head, unable to continue.

"Yes, you should." He pressed his fist into his palm to keep from touching her again, to keep from comforting her with his hands or his mouth. He opened the door and they walked back to the house side by side without touching.

"We're both tired," she said. "What about those beans?"

"They have to cook all day. I'll start them tomorrow morning."

She glanced at him sideways. Tomorrow . . . Tomorrow morning and tomorrow night. It was no longer a question of whether he was staying, it was a question of how long and where. She couldn't keep him on the couch any longer with Grandma and Grandpa's four-poster empty in the other bedroom. Not if he was going to stay one more . . . two more nights.

"I've got a chicken in the refrigerator."

"Sounds like Southern-fried chicken."

She shook her head. "It's my turn to cook. I do know how. Grandma made sure of that. She always made chicken and dumplings in the winter."

"All right," he said, holding the back door open for her. "You talked me into it."

She left her jacket on the back of a kitchen chair and reached into the refrigerator for the chicken. "Now leave me alone for a few minutes so I can concentrate. If I don't get the dumplings just right they fall like rocks." With her hands in the flour, she said, "You're covered with mud. Why don't you run a bath upstairs in the tub? Grandpa's straight-edge razor is in the cabinet and there are clean overalls in his closet."

She heard him take the steps two at a time as she measured baking powder. A half hour later she was chopping onions and carrots when she heard Max come thumping back down the stairs. Without turning from the chopping block she caught a whiff of pine-scented bath soap.

"How was it?" she asked.

She felt his hand on her shoulder, his touch so warm and so sensual that her stomach did a double somersault. She wanted to turn, to bury her head against his chest and stay there while he stroked her shoulders and then her back, but she didn't. She continued her chopping until her hand hurt.

"It was fine," he answered at last.

Still she didn't look at him. "Did you find everything?"

"Mmm-hmm."

"Overalls fit?"

"What do you think?"

Reluctantly she turned to see him in Grandpa's collarless striped shirt and wide blue jeans, so wide they had to be held up by Grandpa's suspenders. She crossed her arms over her chest and gave in to the urge to chuckle. She shook her head and let the laughter bubble out of her lips.

His lower lip jutted out as he hooked his thumbs in his pockets. "What's so funny? I'll bet you didn't laugh when your grandfather dressed like this."

She shook her head. "No, we didn't. But he'd be glad to see you getting some use out of his clothes. He hated waste."

"A true Yankee."

She found herself staring at the sharp contours of Max's clean-shaven face, wanting to run her finger along his jaw to see if it felt as smooth as it looked. He followed her gaze.

"What's wrong, did I cut myself?"

"No," she said and turned back to shaping the dough for the dumplings.

He straddled a straight-backed pine chair and leaned forward to watch her. "Smells good."

"That's the chicken."

"I know."

Suddenly she turned to face him, her hands coated with flour. "I really appreciate what you did today. I couldn't have done it alone."

"Sure you could, you just couldn't have done it as fast."

"How can I repay you?" she asked. She knew what some men would want and what they would say.

"How about a jar of syrup?"

"That's all?"

"I'd never ask for more than you're willing to give."

Reassured, she went back to the stove to drop the dumplings onto the rich chicken broth. They weren't quite as light as Grandma's, but later, when all was cooked and served, Max ate three helpings, saying Yankee food had been underrated. After dinner they went into the living room, carefully sat on opposite ends of the couch and watched the fire in the fireplace, muscles aching, in a comfortable silence.

Miranda finally brought up the subject of the empty four-poster in the other bedroom, the one next to hers. He said the couch was fine, but she insisted, knowing it wasn't. She yawned and went up the stairs ahead of him. With her hair pinned up on top of her head she soaked in the long porcelain claw-foot tub, picturing Max, the last person who'd been there, running the same soap over his broad shoulders, across his chest . . .

It wasn't her idea to have him stay there for the weekend. It wasn't her idea and it wasn't a good idea, no matter how many jars of syrup they bottled. He was too helpful, too considerate, too good-looking even with a five-o'clock shadow. She couldn't have imagined how anyone could look sexy in Grandpa's suspenders, but Max did. He made her want what she couldn't have, someone to share the work with, someone to share her bed with and someone to share the rest of her life, the way Grandma had had.

She scrubbed her back briskly with a loofah. This man was not a farmer. He was a meteorologist amusing himself for one weekend in the country. His place was not here on the flat farmlands, but high on top of a mountain mixing it up with the world's worst weather. And that's where he'd be on Monday, or the next Monday, gone for good, out of her life forever, and not a moment too soon.

Many more days like this followed by nights like this and she would be helpless to stop the yearning, the longing that she felt when he looked at her or touched her. How long would it be before she made a fool of herself and threw herself at him?

Just let me get through one more day, she prayed. Let me concentrate on the work and not the man. Let him be cranky or irritable and let him look ugly for a change. And take away that Southern drawl! She slid down until the water rose to her chin, squeezed her eyes shut and promised herself she would be strong.

The next day went just as she'd planned. Miranda stayed in the shack, Max worked the trees with the horses. They had the system down so well she bottled even more syrup than the day before. She stumbled out of the shack at the end of the day, more tired than the day before, and went to find Max, who was taking the last bucket from the last tree.

Concerned by the frayed condition of the leather he was going to fasten it to, she reached up to the horse's flank to test it with her fingers. Suddenly the leather snapped apart in her hands, sending the bucket flying and the syrup spilling all over the ground. The horse whinnied and stepped away from the tree. Her giant front hoof landed on Miranda's foot.

She inhaled sharply and doubled over with pain.

"Good God," Max shouted, pulling her up with his hands under her arms. "What happened?"

"Gretel stepped on my foot," she gasped. "My fault for spooking her."

"Let's get back to the house." He scooped her up in his arms and trudged back through the mud. With her teeth clenched, she buried her head against his denim jacket. In the kitchen he set her down on a chair and gently stretched her legs out in front of her on another chair. She threw her head back, trying not to wince as he peeled her boot and then her sock off the injured foot. He ran his fingers up around the anklebone and she sucked in her breath and gripped the edge of the chair with her gloved fingers. One corner of her brain registered the smell of baked beans laced with maple syrup coming from the oven.

"That harness is as old as I am. I should have known..."

"Relax. Don't think about it. I'm going to pack it with ice, see if we can keep the swelling down."

She shivered. "Do you have to?"

"Have to, no, should, yes." Carefully he pulled her jacket from her shoulders and before she could protest he brought the blanket from the hall closet and wrapped it around her. Then he went to the living room and came back with a glass of mulberry wine. "Medicinal purposes," he said, worry lines creasing his face.

She lifted her arm, took a sip of wine, then reached for his hand. "I'm okay, really. It's probably just a sprain and I'll be fine."

He squeezed her hand reassuringly and smiled down at her. "Sure you will. I'll get the ice."

Carefully he lifted her feet off the chair so he could sit on it. He took her foot in one hand, the ice, encased in a plastic bag, in the other. She wiggled her toes and they felt puffy and swollen. Closing her eyes, she leaned her head back against the solid pine backrest. For several minutes he held the plastic bag against her foot, cushioning her soles against his warm chest.

He looked out the kitchen window. "I ought to put the horses in. Can you hold this yourself?"

Her eyes flew open. "Of course." She reached for the ice pack. "I'm not completely helpless."

"If eight hundred pounds of horse had stepped on me, I'd be helpless and you'd be holding my feet and icing my ankle, wouldn't you?"

She nodded, her eyes tearing from the pain and the frustration of being hurt. Now of all times, now when she needed to be strong and healthy.

"Miranda," he said, standing at the back door. "You're going to be all right."

She gave him a watery smile and he closed the door behind him. She told herself he was right, she would be fine, but when? When he came back he wrapped her foot and ankle in a gauze bandage he'd found in the medicine chest in the bathroom. He gave her two aspirin and then dinner in the kitchen, her leg still propped on the chair. She was overwhelmed by his thoughtfulness, confused by his taking charge and rattled by his physical presence. The closer he got the more helpless she felt.

When she finished the last baked bean on her plate, her foot was numb and so was her brain. He reached for her plate and put it into the sink. "How are you doing?"

"Feeling no pain," she said through stiff lips.

"Good. Where's the nearest doctor?"

"On Main Street, why?"

"Because I'm taking you in to see him in the morning."

"What can he do?"

"Take an X ray, bandage it properly." He put water on the stove to boil for coffee.

"I'll be late for work, they're picky about that," she protested.

"We'll get an early start."

"Now wait a minute. You're going home tomorrow. I can get myself there."

"No, you can't."

"I don't like depending on somebody else."

"Neither do I, but all I'm doing is driving you to town. If it were me . . ."

"I know. I'd be driving you to the doctor and making your coffee . . ."

"And carrying me upstairs to bed?" he challenged her with a gleam in his eye.

"Oh, no." She was sinking deeper and deeper into a black hole of depression. If she couldn't even get up the stairs by herself . . .

"You wouldn't?"

"Of course I would if I could, but I bet you wouldn't like being babied any more than I do."

He crossed his arms over his chest and grinned at her. "I'd let you carry me up to bed anytime you want. I'd even let you kiss me good-night if you insisted."

She bit her lip to keep from laughing or crying, she wasn't sure which. "All right."

"All right, you'll kiss me good-night?"

"All right, I'll go to the doctor."

The look in his eyes made her heart skip a beat. Was it so wrong to want to kiss him good-night? She knew how his lips would feel on hers, warm and firm. He crossed the room, lifted her and carried her up the stairs. With her arms around his neck, her cheek was pressed against his.

"Max," she gasped, "I'm too much for you."

"You're right," he said, backing onto her feather bed and cradling her tightly to him. "Way too much." He rolled on his back, cushioning her and sinking deeper onto the soft billows of the bed, one arm around her shoulders, the other on her round bottom. She turned to roll out of his arms and landed on top of him, her breasts pressed against his chest, her bandaged foot in the air, feeling ridiculous, but so relaxed and so mellow she didn't care.

"Come here," he muttered.

"Where?" she asked. But she knew. Their lips met somewhere between heaven and earth and she forgot about her foot, forgot about the syrup, forgot about everything but Max and the fire he kindled deep within her. Outside the wind came up and the temperature fell to below freezing, but inside she felt the heat from his body, heard his heart pound, and felt her heart match his, beat for beat.

He cradled her face in his hands, his hunger for her growing stronger with every kiss, until he knew he'd never get enough, not tonight, not ever. He rolled onto his side, taking her with him, and she moaned, bringing him to his senses at last. "I hurt you. I'm sorry. Got to get you to bed."

Dazed, she looked around. "I am in bed."

He sat up and looked down at her, at her hair tangled and fanned out around her face, her eyes unfocused, her lips as soft and dewy as dawn. But it wasn't dawn, it was night and she ought to be in her bed instead of on top of it. His heart contracted. What kind of a jerk would take advantage of her immobility and her weakness? She'd kissed him, yes. And he'd felt her hunger, her desire leap to match his own. But how much of that was the painkiller, the wine and the TLC? Most of it, he suspected ruefully. He stood at the side of the bed. "Where's your nightgown?"

She pointed to the chair in the corner and he tossed the soft pink garment to her. If he didn't get out of her room soon he'd be undressing her, sliding her shirt over her head, pulling those flannel pants off her hips and settling the nightgown over her head, the soft cotton caressing her breasts as it drifted over her body and covered her long legs. He paused in the doorway.

"Do you need anything else?" he asked in a voice that sounded more like gravel than anything else.

She shook her head and he closed the door behind him.

Chapter Five

The throbbing in her foot woke her up, as well as the smell of coffee and the sizzle of bacon from the kitchen. Her mouth watered, her stomach contracted. It was a good thing he was leaving today. Baked beans, pancakes and now bacon. She could get used to this. Usually she raced out of the house with no time for breakfast, only time to empty the buckets. She slapped her palm against her forehead. She'd almost forgotten the buckets and the sap. She slid out of bed and winced as the blood went to her foot and made it pound. After putting on her quilted robe, she sat down on the top of the landing and took the stairs one step at a time on her bottom.

He heard her coming and met her as she hit the last step. "Where do you think you're going?" he asked.

She tilted her head, her eyes traveling slowly up the narrow hip-hugging blue jeans he'd arrived in, now free of mud, then across his thick natural wool sweater and finally, reluctantly, met his blue-eyed gaze. The kiss, the roll on the bed was not forgotten. It was there between them.

She felt it. He must feel it, too. She swallowed hard. "I'm going out to collect the sap as soon as I get dressed, why?"

He lowered himself to her level and looked her straight in the eye. "It's done."

"Why didn't you tell me?"

"You were asleep."

Her forehead creased into a frown. "You're taking over my farm, my kitchen and my life. What am I going to do with you?" she asked mournfully.

"The question is what are you going to do without me?" he asked, bending his knees and picking her up in his arms.

"I'll manage," she said, resisting the urge to throw her arms around his neck. He set her down on the kitchen chair and served her a rasher of bacon and hot buttered toast.

"How's your foot?" he asked, taking the chair opposite hers and pouring a liberal amount of cream into his coffee.

"Fine," she lied.

"I'm sorry about last night," he said, looking at her over the rim of the thick mug. "I forgot about your foot."

She concentrated on her toast. "Me, too." It was true. She'd forgotten about her foot, but she hadn't forgotten the reckless abandon that had overwhelmed her, the warmth of his gaze turning hot with passion, but she wasn't sorry, although she probably should have been.

She was only sorry it had ended so abruptly with his tossing her nightgown at her. Either he had suddenly lost interest or he had more control than she did. She found herself staring at him this morning, but the look in his eyes told her nothing. He looked at her with concern, but no more than you'd show any friend whose foot had been stepped on by a horse. And instead of putting up another fight, she might as well let him drive her to the doctor if he wanted to. She didn't look forward to tromping on the clutch in her truck with her aching foot.

After breakfast he brought his car close to the front porch. When she got dressed she left the house and hobbled down the steps with her swollen foot in a slipper and got into the front seat. And thanked him again.

"All I ever do is thank you," she sighed, her head tilted back on the padded headrest.

"You can stop now. I don't want to be thanked."

She slanted a curious glance in his direction. "What do you want?"

He looked at her for a few brief seconds before turning his attention to the pockmarked road ahead. What did he want? He knew what he didn't want. He didn't want to return to his empty apartment and spend the week thinking about her and her syrup and her horses and her foot. "To see you get back on your feet again," he said finally. There, that said it all and yet said nothing.

They didn't speak again until they got to Main Street and she directed him to the doctor's office. He parked and followed her up the stairs. The doctor wasn't due for another fifteen minutes and the waiting room was half full of people Miranda seemed to know. After she greeted them, she looked at her watch.

"Don't tell me they don't give you any sick leave," he said from behind the magazine he was holding in front of his face.

"I'm going to use my sick leave to work on the farm," she said. "I'm not going to waste it being sick." Impatiently she started to stand up and pace around the office, but he pulled her down by the arm. She glared at him and then picked up an old farmer's almanac and thumbed through the pages. "I'll give him ten more minutes," she said under her breath. But it was another half hour before the receptionist called her name and yet another before she reappeared in the waiting room. By that time he'd read and reread the same article three times and hadn't understood a single word. When he saw her emerge from the examination room her face was almost as white as the piece of paper she was clutching in her hand.

He put his hands on her shoulders. "What is it, what did he say?"

He felt the eyes of the other patients watching them and he saw her face flush with embarrassment. She turned quickly and walked out of the office while he followed on her heels.

"It's nothing. I just tore a few ligaments," she said over her shoulder.

"No broken bones?"

"No."

"What's the prescription for?" They were on the street now, heading toward the car.

"Painkiller."

"Are you in pain?"

"No, but if I am, I'll get it filled."

He took it out of her hand. "I'll get it filled for you. Did you ask if you could go to work?"

"Of course I can go to work. As long as I keep my foot up."

"Then what are you standing there for?" He let go of her hand and settling her in the car, drove the two blocks to the Green Merchants building, pulling up to the employee entrance. Before he'd come to a complete stop she was opening the door and getting ready to get out.

"Thanks for the ride," she said, then shook her head, realizing what she'd done—thanked him again. "Have a safe trip home."

"I'll be back with the pills."

She nodded. "You can leave them at the front desk." She closed the car door to avoid the look in his eyes, a shuttered look that made her ashamed of dismissing him as if he were her chauffeur. She told herself it was the pain and the anxiety that made her act that way, but underneath the pain was the fear that she'd become too attached to Max and too dependent on his help. Besides the obvious questions that swirled around in her head, such as how to collect syrup while staying off her foot and how to think about lost parcels and broken knapsacks and cope with the pain that wouldn't go away, was the big question. How was she going to get along without him?

It wasn't the work. She could hire someone to help her. It was the emotional support he provided, the kindness and the care he took with her and the farm. That kind of help couldn't be hired.

By the time she reached her desk, Miranda had answered the question "What happened to your foot?" about a dozen times, received solicitous advice and offers for everything from a wheelchair to chicken soup. Exhausted, she fell into her chair and gratefully accepted a makeshift footrest from Lianne and Mavis before she started on the problems piled on her desk.

At lunchtime when the others left, Ariel appeared, bearing two huge deli sandwiches stacked high with thinly sliced corned beef on rye, cartons of potato salad and two bottles of fruit-flavored mineral water. Miranda switched on her answering machine, shoved the orders to one side and turned in her chair to face her sister.

"I can't believe what happened to you," Ariel said.

"How did you hear?"

"I'd have to be deaf not to hear. Everyone's talking about your foot and the fact that Max spent the weekend with you."

Miranda squeezed her eyes shut. *"Oh, no."*

"Oh, *yes*. Why, is it a secret?"

"No, of course it's not a secret. I just don't like being the subject of gossip."

"It's a small town."

"No kidding. You should have seen the open mouths at the doctor's office this morning."

"What did he say?"

"Stay off my foot."

Ariel shook her head. "I mean Max."

"The same thing. Stay off my foot."

Ariel unwrapped her sandwich. "All weekend long, that's all he said?"

Miranda chewed hungrily. The pain in her foot hadn't affected her appetite. "We were too busy working to talk. We bottled four dozen jars between us."

Ariel's eyes widened in admiration. "The man is too good to be true. Looks like an all-American and works like a Trojan. What else?" she demanded.

Miranda set her sandwich down. "Isn't that enough?"

Ariel shrugged. "If you say so."

"I do say so. What are you getting at, as if I didn't know?"

Ariel looked around and lowered her voice. "There's absolutely no one within one hundred feet. You can tell me what really happened. I'm your sister, for heaven's sake."

Miranda slid her chair toward her sister, holding a plastic spoon in one hand and her carton of potato salad in the other. *"He cooked,"* she said in a stage whisper, "and then, after dinner . . ." She paused dramatically.

"Yes, go on."

"We went to bed."

"Where?"

"Upstairs."

Ariel edged her chair closer to Miranda's. "Are you serious?"

"You don't think I'd make him sleep on the couch, do you, after all he'd done for me?"

Speechless, Ariel shook her head. "I can't believe it," she said at last.

"Can't believe I'd let him sleep in Grandma's four-poster?"

Ariel blinked. "Where did you sleep?"

"In my bed."

"But what happened, before you went to sleep?"

"You mean after he carried me up to bed?"

Ariel gasped. "He carried you up the stairs? That is the most romantic thing I've ever heard. What happened next?"

"He put me down on my bed, and..." She lifted her gaze over Ariel's head. "Oh, hello, Mr. Northwood."

Ariel choked with suppressed laughter. "Don't try that one on me, it won't work. There's no one here but us and I'm not leaving until I've heard the whole story from..."

"Excuse me, ladies. May I have a word with you, Miranda?" The raspy voice of the owner of Green Mountain Merchants caused Ariel to rise out of her chair like a marionette on strings. Turning a bright fuchsia, the exact color of her sweater, she swept her half-eaten sandwich off the console and made as graceful an exit as possible.

Miranda watched her go, the urge to laugh conflicting with the urge to cry. She hadn't seen Mr. Northwood for days. Why now, when she was feeling so awful, and so behind in her work?

"I understand you've had an accident." His narrow, flint-gray eyes skimmed her bandaged foot stretched out on the chair in front of her.

"It's nothing, really. Just a little sprain," she said, forcing a cheerful smile.

"If it prevents you from working..."

"It doesn't," she assured him.

"Feel free to use your sick days, three of which have accrued so far, I believe."

"Thank you, but it won't be necessary."

"Then you feel ready to buckle down, to solve the various problems that are part and parcel of our business, so to speak?"

"Oh, I do, I definitely do." What was the man getting at? Or was he just making the rounds, seeing who was eating lunch at their desks and who wasn't?

"Good." He pressed his gnarled fingers together and cracked his knuckles. Miranda winced. "Then perhaps you can explain this discrepancy to me.'' He spread several blue order forms in front of her on her desk, all of which were orders for fleece-lined all-weather boots to be sent to one Maxwell Carter in care of the Mount Henry Weather Station, Mount Henry, New Hampshire. ''Three sets of boots sent to the same party, but only one bill sent, and only one bill paid.'' He waved the invoice in front of her.

The words on the paper swam in front of her eyes, but she didn't have to see them to know what they said. Explain it? ''Yes, of course. If you'll give me a few minutes to track it down. It's just a little mix-up, a slight misunderstanding.'' She shuffled the papers in front of her, waiting for him to leave so she could put her head on her desk and burst into tears. Because the truth was there was no mix-up or misunderstanding. There were two pairs of boots missing, gone, disappeared from the face of the earth and nobody was going to pay for them.

''I'll be in my office,'' he said, ''waiting for your explanation. As soon as you solve this 'little mix-up' let me know.'' After receiving another reassuring smile from Miranda, Mr. Northwood padded away as silently as he'd arrived. Instead of bursting into tears, Miranda opened her bottom file drawer and pulled out file after file folder, looking into them for some clue and putting them back again.

The rest of her department came back from lunch. Mavis set a package from the pharmacy in front of her. ''It was at the front desk,'' she said. Miranda nodded but she scarcely looked up. She called the shipping department. They insisted they'd sent the first pair by overnight mail, and she knew she'd sent the others herself. Five o'clock came and the other women got ready to leave but Miranda wasn't any closer to an answer than she'd been at noon.

Mavis tossed her scarf over her shoulder. ''Miranda, give up. I tell you, I spent hours trying to track down those boots when your friend first complained about them a million years ago. They're gone, believe me. Old man North-wood's just going to have to stuff it."

"I know, I know. I just have one more place to look...."

"Need a ride home?"

"No, thanks. I'll catch a ride with Howard. He goes my way."

Mavis arched one eyebrow. "Howard or that marvelous hunk who brought you in this morning?"

Miranda shook her head. "He's gone back to New Hampshire."

"Too bad."

The office was eerily quiet after Mavis left, but her words reverberated through the empty room. "Too bad, too bad, too bad." Was that the real reason she was postponing going home, that there was no one to go home to? How ridiculous. It occurred to her that maybe Mr. Northwood had gone, too. She limped to the employee entrance and peered through the dusk into the parking lot. Mr. Northwood's car was still there and one other, Max's sedan. Her heart jolted. She leaned against the door, not knowing whether to run and hide or open the door and call his name.

So she did neither. Out of the winter twilight he came up the steps without her calling him and looked at her through the double pane of glass that separated them. His hair was dusted with snow, his breath came in puffs of vapor and his eyes bored into hers, those piercing blue eyes that turned her knees to jelly. She turned the doorknob and he stepped in.

"I thought you went home," she said.

"I did. I picked up some things and I came back. I can give you a ride home."

She staggered backward. He'd gone to New Hampshire and come back to give her a ride home? It didn't make sense. Maybe it didn't have to. He was here and she was glad to see him. Glad to hear his voice, glad to feel the warmth that his presence generated.

"That's nice," she said, "but I can't go yet. Not until I figure out what happened to your lost boots."

"My lost boots? Don't worry about it, it's my problem."

"No, it's Mr. Northwood's problem, because there are two pairs of missing boots and they haven't been paid for."

"I'll pay for them."

"That's not fair. You didn't get them."

"They'll turn up," he assured her. "I have faith in the U.S. Post Office. I read the other day a man in Texas just got a letter from his nephew who fought in World War II. It was dated 1943."

"But if they turn up you'll have three pairs of the same boots."

"That's fine with me. I can always use them."

"Oh, Max." How could anybody be so good-looking and so nice? She felt her knees buckle.

He grabbed her under the arms and held her upright. "What are you doing on your feet? Did you take your medicine?"

She shook her head. "I've been too busy."

"Let's get out of here."

"I'll go tell Mr. Northwood."

He waited for her in the employee lunchroom, wondering how he was going to tell her he was planning to stay all week. He had his bag in his trunk and nothing to do this week. Normally he'd repair broken equipment in his apartment in town and wait for Monday. He knew he should have another life, but he didn't want one. It made sense to him to spend the week helping her process sap. She couldn't do it; he could. He liked the farm, the trees and the snow and the quiet nights in that four-poster bed where he lay trying not to think about her.

The whole house with its peeling paint, sagging furniture and old-fashioned cookstove wove a spell around him like a cocoon. Maybe she didn't feel it, the house was her home and she was used to it. But he'd never had a home of his own. A home was too much work, too distracting and too demanding. Like a woman, come to think of it. The advantages of having either one hadn't entered his mind for a long time.

She came back with her navy blue anorak over her shoulders, accentuating her soft honey-blond hair. There was a look on her face he couldn't decipher. It was partly relief mixed with anticipation and a touch of anxiety. What could he say to dispel the anxiety and encourage the anticipation of spending the week with him? He'd promise her anything she wanted.

No more kisses or trips across the hall to her bedroom. He'd already promised himself that much. He didn't trust himself any more unless he restricted himself to all work and no play. She'd be relieved to hear that. Or would she be more relieved to see him drive away into the sunset once and for all?

Even if she didn't want him around, she might put up with him just to get the sap processed. He thought he could count on that. And that was all he wanted. When he pulled up in front of the farmhouse, she turned to face him. It made his heart turn over to see the fatigue lurking at the corners of her eyes. He wanted to soothe the hurt away, but he kept his hands wrapped around the steering wheel.

"Sure you don't want to take some of those sick days?" he asked.

She stiffened. "You and Mr. Northwood. No, I don't. I'm not sick." She put her hand on his arm. "Max, don't tell me you drove all the way back here just to give me a ride home."

He smiled into her dark, troubled eyes. "No, I didn't. I was hoping you'd invite me to dinner. I want to talk to you."

Tiny worry lines formed between her eyebrows, then she gave him a tentative smile. "Come on in, but I'm afraid the cupboard's bare."

He opened the front door for her. "I was thinking about making an omelet. I picked up some mushrooms along the way."

"I'll help," she said, throwing her jacket on the couch.

"You break the eggs while I empty the buckets and feed the horses," he said. And he left before she could protest.

The buckets were overflowing by the time he got to them. He left the sap in the shack, where he planned to take charge of the boiling tomorrow when she went off to work at Green Mountain. If she went off to work. If she let him stay.

When he got back to the kitchen, he took over, impressing her by flipping the omelet high in the air before it settled back in the pan. He was no good at small talk so they ate in silence while he waited for the right moment to break the news to her.

"How's your foot?" he asked as she ate the last mushroom on her plate.

"Fine," she answered automatically. "What did you want to talk about?"

"What are you going to do about the syrup?"

Her eyes narrowed. "What do you mean?"

"I mean you can't do it all, work in town and work here. You never could."

Her eyes blazed. "I could, too."

He ignored her outburst. "With your foot you shouldn't do anything but stay home and let it heal."

"You're not the doctor."

"I've seen lots of accidents, from skiing and mountain climbing. I know what torn ligaments are. I've even torn a few myself."

"And what did you do, sit quietly and let them heal?"

He leaned forward across the table. "I did when I broke my leg. I didn't enjoy it, but I did it."

"I'm going to work, Max. I have to. I can't afford to take sick leave. As for the syrup..." She rubbed her hand across her forehead. "I don't know what to do."

"I'll do it. I saw what you did in the shack. I can haul it and boil it down by myself."

"Why would you want to do that?"

Now came the hard part. How to explain something he didn't fully understand himself. "I enjoy the work. And if you're worried about what happened last night happening again, well it won't. I guarantee it."

A slow flush crept up her neck. "I wasn't . . . I didn't . . . I don't know what to say. I'm overwhelmed."

"Say yes."

"If I do, how can I repay you?"

He smelled victory. "In syrup?"

She sighed. "If I gave it all to you, it still wouldn't be enough. This is the second time you've bailed me out today. There must be something you want, something I could give you."

Restless, he stood and leaned against the Formica counter and thought about it. There was so much she had to give and so much he wanted to take. But it was not for him to say. He thought about carrying her up the stairs to bed again. He'd have to leave her on the bed without touching her, or else he couldn't stay here. She was looking at him, waiting for his answer. He dredged his mind and came up blank. He couldn't remember the question.

"Something I want?" he said at last. "Not really. I've got everything I need. Completely self-sufficient." It sounded smug, but it was true. His job was the most important thing in his life and as long as he had it he didn't need or want anything else.

She propped her elbows on the table, cupped her chin in her palm and regarded him out of her luminous dark eyes. "I envy you. I wish I could be more like that."

He shifted uncomfortably under her gaze. "You shouldn't envy anyone. You've got a house to come home to, and not just any house, one that's been in your family for years." He looked around at the open cupboards, the hand-painted design on the molding. "You've got friends and family who all care about you...." The more he said the worse he felt, thinking of everything she had and he didn't. He stopped and gave her a rueful smile. "Well, now that we have that settled, it's past your bedtime."

She looked up at him under heavy eyelids, too tired to protest. He crossed the room in two steps and swept her up. He felt her arms go around his neck, her hand tangle in his hair and his knees almost gave way on the first step. He thought he could do it, but he hadn't counted on the faint smell of flowers that clung to her hair, or the touch of her fingers on the back of his neck. He inhaled deeply and, with a rush of adrenaline, took the stairs two at a time. He set her on the edge of her bed and quickly left the room, closing the door behind him. There was only so much a man could take.

The week ahead tested his resolve every day in every way. Before he drove her to work every morning he was forced to see how she looked before she'd had her coffee, before she'd applied any makeup or combed her hair. He saw her at her worst and he couldn't tear his eyes away. And at night, after they'd sat in front of the fire talking, he'd run into her on her way out of the bath, her skin moist and dewy, her hair pinned up, hanging in damp tendrils around her face, and he had to go into his room—her grandparents' room— throw himself on the bed and grind his teeth in frustration.

He tried not to look at her. But he couldn't stop imagining how it would feel if she were next to him in that four-poster on cold winter nights such as these. But he'd promised her it wouldn't happen, and as long as he was under her roof, it wouldn't. That didn't stop him from dreaming, though, at night and during the day. He dreamed of getting into the deep, claw-foot tub with her, he dreamed of taking that nightgown off or putting it on her and that was the kind of thing that kept him awake at night.

NO RISK, NO OBLIGATION TO BUY...NOW OR EVER!

CASINO JUBILEE
"Scratch'n Match" Game

Here's how to play:

1. Peel off label from front cover. Place it in space provided at right. With a coin, carefully scratch off the silver box. This makes you eligible to receive two or more free books, and possibly another gift, depending upon what is revealed beneath the scratch-off area.

2. Send back this card and you'll receive brand-new Silhouette Romance™ novels. These books have a cover price of $2.75 each, but they are yours to keep absolutely free.

3. There's no catch. You're under no obligation to buy anything. We charge nothing – ZERO – for your first shipment. And you don't have to make any minimum number of purchases – not even one!

4. The fact is thousands of readers enjoy receiving books by mail from the Silhouette Reader Service™ months before they're available in stores. They like the convenience of home delivery and they love our discount prices!

5. We hope that after receiving your free books you'll want to remain a subscriber. But the choice is yours – to continue or cancel, anytime at all! So why not take us up on our invitation, with no risk of any kind. You'll be glad you did!

YOURS FREE! ▶ *This lovely Victorian pewter-finish miniature is perfect for displaying a treasured photograph – and it's yours absolutely free – when you accept our no-risk offer.*

CASINO JUBILEE
"Scratch'n Match" Game

CHECK CLAIM CHART BELOW
FOR YOUR FREE GIFTS!

YES! I have placed my label from the front cover in the space provided above and scratched off the silver box. Please send me all the gifts for which I qualify. I understand that I am under no obligation to purchase any books, as explained on the back and on the opposite page.

215 CIS AKYN (U-SIL-R-08/93)

Name _____

Address _____ Apt._____

City _____ State _____ Zip_____

CASINO JUBILEE CLAIM CHART	
🍒🍒🍒 🍒🍒🍒	WORTH 4 FREE BOOKS AND A FREE VICTORIAN PICTURE FRAME
🍒🍒🍒 🍒🔔🍒	WORTH 4 FREE BOOKS
🔔🔔🔔 🍒🍒🍒	WORTH 3 FREE BOOKS CLAIM N° 1528

Offer limited to one per household and not valid to current Silhouette Romance™ subscribers. All orders subject to approval.

▼ DETACH AND MAIL CARD TODAY! ▼

THE SILHOUETTE READER SERVICE™ : HERE'S HOW IT WORKS

Accepting free books puts you under no obligation to buy anything. You may keep the books and gift and return the shipping statement marked "cancel." If you do not cancel, about a month later we will send you 6 additional novels and bill you just $1.99 each plus 25¢ delivery and applicable sales tax, if any.* That's the complete price, and – compared to cover prices of $2.75 each – quite a bargain! You may cancel at any time, but if you choose to continue, every month we'll send you 6 more books, which you may either purchase at the discount price... or return at our expense and cancel your subscription.

*Terms and prices subject to change without notice. Sales tax applicable in N.Y.

It was almost a relief when the week came to an end. Miranda's foot was almost healed, the sap had almost stopped running and he had almost run out of self-control. He'd processed hundreds of bottles of syrup and on the last run on Sunday afternoon, he and Miranda had each rode one of the horses back to the barn for a well-earned rest. He arrived first, lowered himself from the broad back of Hans, the larger of the two plodding draft horses, and waited by the barn for Miranda to come in from the field on Gretel. Mud from the horse's hooves spattered onto his jeans as she pulled up in front of him. He held out his arms to help her down and she slid into them as easily as warm maple syrup flowed from a pitcher.

For just a moment she stayed there, in the circle of his arms, her eyes full of questions he couldn't answer. She knew, they both knew it was over, this week of living together, of playing house. What they didn't know was what came next. Was it really over, this intimate sharing of their lives? Or was this only the beginning of something deeper and more meaningful? Whatever happened next, they both knew things would never be the same.

Instead of gathering her in his arms and telling her what he wanted, which was impossible because he didn't know what he wanted, he dropped his arms abruptly and said goodbye.

The color drained from her face for a moment, then she recovered. "I thought you were staying for dinner."

He shook his head, feeling remorse clog his throat. "Can't do it, not tonight. Some other time. I've got to get back."

It was a lame excuse and she knew it. Her lips trembled and she turned toward her horse to hide her face. "Of course. Well, don't forget to take the syrup I owe you."

"I won't." Why was he doing this, walking out on her after the most incredible week of his life? Because he was scared, so scared his hands shook as he slapped the horse on its flank. Scared of hurting her and of getting hurt. Scared of getting involved and of involving her. "Miranda?"

She looked over her shoulder. "Yes?"

"I'll get my stuff from the house. Take care."

Her eyes were suspiciously bright. "Thanks...for everything."

He walked in the back door, picked up his bag from the bedroom upstairs and hurried down the stairs and out the front door. He got into his car and pulled away from the old house before he changed his mind and broke his promise to her and to himself.

Chapter Six

Miranda sat on the couch in front of the fireplace staring at the ashes that lay there, cold and lifeless, from other nights and other fires. When Max had been there. Outside the wind was blowing and the temperature was falling. She ought to build a fire. She ought to make dinner. But what was the point? She had no one to eat with, no one to sit with in front of the fire and talk with about everything and nothing.

She told herself to stop wallowing in self-pity. She told herself to snap out of it. But she might as well have been talking to the wall. She would wallow to her heart's content tonight and tomorrow she'd be her old self, full of hope and optimism and independence. She just needed a short period of adjustment, to adjust from having someone around to having no one. Not that she needed someone. Not Miranda Morrison who ran a farm with one hand and handled complaints at a mail-order company with the other.

She stretched her feet out in front of her toward the cold brick hearth and wiggled her toes. If it hadn't been for her accident, she would have bottled all that syrup herself and never missed having a helper, a partner, a . . . a friend. But she had torn her ligaments and she'd had the most thoughtful, most desirable man with the bluest eyes, the broadest shoulders, the strongest arms. . . .

Not that she'd noticed how first thing in the morning his blond hair would be standing on end, the shadow of a beard grazing his jaw. And she'd almost forgotten what he looked like on his way to the bathroom without a shirt, wearing only sweatpants, the cord around his waist knotted low on his flat stomach. Sitting there alone in the living room she felt her pulse race just remembering. It was only natural to feel something after a week of living together. Even if it was only relief. Yes, that's what it was, relief to have him gone, to have the house to herself again. Not to have to pick up his wet towel from the bathroom floor. Not to have to eat his Southern-fried chicken, or the grits he made for breakfast on a cold winter morning with sausage and country gravy.

It was back to canned soup for dinner and a cup of coffee in the morning. It was all over, the sapping season, the sharing and the caring. That was obvious from the way he'd said goodbye. As if he could hardly wait to get away. She couldn't blame him. He'd worked hard, taken care of the farm and her, too. Why? What did he get out of it? He'd even forgotten the few jars of syrup she'd promised him. There were times during the week when she'd caught him glancing at her, a quizzical look in his eyes, as if he, too, wondered what he was doing there.

And then there was that night, the first night he'd carried her up to bed when she'd thought, had even hoped he wouldn't leave her. But he had, he always did. Why shouldn't he? This wasn't his farm or his life. His life was hundreds of miles away, thousands of feet in the sky, watching the clouds and measuring the snowfall.

She shivered as night fell around the farm, unwilling to turn up the heat or turn on the lights. Why bother if it was just for her? Why bother doing anything? After a while she climbed the stairs and went to bed.

It was better at work. In the days that followed she had to forget about herself and think of others, like the lady whose angora polo pullover shrunk when she put it in the dryer. Miranda sent her another one and cautioned her to read the instructions on the label. She gossiped with the other women and went to lunch with her sister. Ariel was surprised she hadn't heard from Max, but noting the expression on Miranda's face, she let it drop and changed the subject.

Miranda wasn't surprised she hadn't heard from him as the weeks passed. Why would he call her? What would he say? Still she found herself wondering if the missing boots had ever turned up. She couldn't call and ask him, not if he didn't call her. But she could call and ask the post office in the town of Mount Henry if they'd arrived.

"Packages for Mr. Carter are held for pickup," the postmistress informed her primly.

"Why is that?"

"You'll have to ask Mr. Carter, since he's the one who requested it. In writing."

"How long ago was that?" Miranda asked.

"I really can't say. I'm new here. I was just transferred from Crawford Notch. And the notice isn't dated."

Miranda frowned. "Are there any packages being held right now?"

"Just a moment, I'll check." There was a long silence while Miranda fidgeted with the buttons on her camel-hair cardigan. "Yes, ma'am," she answered at last.

"Could you tell me, are any of them from Green Mountain Merchants?"

"All of them."

"How late are you open?"

"Until five."

Miranda grabbed her fleece-lined jacket, striped wool hat and gloves, and headed for the door, leaving Mavis and

Lianne and Donna and Penny staring after her with their mouths hanging open in surprise.

"Cover for me, will you?" she called over her shoulder and they looked at each other in bewilderment.

"There she goes again," Donna murmured.

"Hasn't been herself lately," Mavis noted.

"Something's got into her," Lianne agreed.

At three o'clock on a Friday afternoon there wasn't much traffic on the road that crossed New Hampshire from Northern Vermont to the White Mountains of New Hampshire. But Miranda wouldn't have noticed if there had been. She had her eyes on the cloud-shrouded mountains in the distance and her mind on the two packages of boots in the Mount Henry Post Office. It was clear her duty to Max was to deliver the boots he'd paid for without delay. How she would do that she had no idea. She couldn't hope to borrow the tractor again.

She arrived at the small post office in the tiny hamlet of Mount Henry at precisely 4:55 and stood in line for the next ten minutes while customers bought stamps and mailed packages, none of which was as important as her mission. After an eternity she reached the window just in time to present her case. "I'm the one who called ... about the packages for Mr. Carter?"

"They can't be released until Mr. Carter comes to pick them up."

"It's okay, he wants the packages. I know he does."

"I'm sorry."

"What if he called and said it was all right?"

"He hasn't." She put her hand on the glass partition and Miranda was afraid she'd close it on her fingers.

"It's a mistake, I know it is. Just let me call him and ask him."

The postmistress sighed. "There's a phone back here on the desk."

Miranda went around to the back through a side door and paused with her hand on the receiver. "I don't suppose you know the number at the observatory?"

The woman rolled her eyes and pointed to a slim telephone book on the desk.

"Thank you. It will only take a minute."

But it took an eternity for him to answer. The phone rang and rang before he finally answered.

"Max, I found your boots," she said breathlessly.

"Really, where?"

"At the post office in Mount Henry. The boots are here and they're about to close. They won't release them to me because you told them to hold all your packages for pickup. That's why they didn't deliver them. They've been here all the time."

"Oh Lord, of course. I remember now. I sent my anemometer in for repair and when it came back it still wasn't fixed. So I told the post office not to send any more packages up here until I came down and checked them out first. But that was months ago."

"Tell the lady it's okay, and I'll bring them up to you."

Miranda held the receiver up so the postmistress could hear Max give his approval, then she heard Max talking to her. "Don't come up, I'm coming down. Stay where you are. I'll meet you there."

Miranda took the boxes and went out the front door, which they locked behind her. She stood looking up and down the street without seeing the houses with their snow-covered peaked roofs. Her mind was whirling, thinking of seeing Max in a few minutes.

She stamped her feet on the snow-packed sidewalk to keep warm until she saw his car coming down the street. Inside her gloves her palms perspired as she saw his tall angular figure get out of the car and cross the sidewalk. He was smiling broadly, a look of anticipation on his face that for a brief moment she thought might be for her, until she remembered the two packages at her feet, the boots he'd been waiting for for so long.

She picked them up and held them out to him. To her surprise he wrapped his arms around her with the packages squashed between them. He brought with him the smell of cold mountain air, of fir trees mixed with his own masculine scent, and her heart began to race. Suddenly she was warm, a radiant warmth deep inside her for the first time since he'd left her weeks ago.

He pulled back and looked deep into her eyes. "I missed you," he said.

She gulped, not knowing whether to admit she'd missed him, too, or to keep up the pretense of self-sufficiency. So she didn't say anything.

Max took the packages out of her arms and dumped them into the trunk of his car. To make room he had to shove his duffel bag and two pairs of short cross-country skis to one side. He stood with his hand on the open trunk door, looking at her for a long moment. "Do you ski?" he asked.

She cleared her throat and found her voice. "Ski? No, I don't."

"You're from Vermont and you don't ski?"

She gave him a half smile. "People from Vermont don't ski," she explained. "They can't afford it. Skiing is for people who come up here from New York, or... Georgia."

"Wouldn't you like to learn?"

"Sure, of course, someday. After I get some extra money for the skis and the boots and the lift ticket and..."

"I was thinking of cross-country. You don't need a lift ticket and I've got an extra pair of skis here for a guy I know. I was supposed to meet him at the lodge at Cranmore, but he had to cancel at the last minute. His wife."

Miranda frowned. "His wife what?"

"Wouldn't let him go. It's always that way. He works at a station in Maine, one week off and one on like me. This is his week off, and she wants him home. And since he doesn't want to end up in divorce court like me he's going home.''

Miranda twisted her fingers together, not knowing what to say. Not knowing who to feel sorrier for, the wife, the husband, or Max, who stood there on the snow-packed sidewalk next to her, looking at the mountains in the distance with a faraway look in his eyes. Deliberately he brought his gaze back to her.

"What I'm getting at is that I've got the extra skis, you can rent boots up there and Jack's already paid for his room and it's too late to get the money back. So I think you should take his place and come with me."

"To Cranmore?" Her voice went up a notch until it turned into a squeak.

"It's not the moon," he assured her. "Cranmore is right here in the White Mountains, only two hours away. What's the matter, is it your foot?"

She shook her head. "My foot's fine, but it's . . . the horses. I've got to get back to feed them." Overnight at a ski resort with Max? Her mind was spinning. Her heart rate was accelerating. She couldn't go. She shouldn't go, but oh, how she wanted to go.

"Can't your sister do it?"

"No, but maybe Howard could. He's my closest neighbor."

Max closed the trunk with a bang. "Call him."

Miranda called him from a pay phone in a drugstore three doors away from the post office and he said he'd feed them. Then she put her car in a parking lot behind the drugstore, bought a few personal items in the store and got into Max's car.

Relaxing in the warm, upholstered interior at last, she studied Max's profile while his attention was on the road. Had his jaw always been so jutting, his hair so thick and soft she wanted to push it back from his forehead? All the pent-up doubts about spending more time with him rose to her throat and threatened to choke her.

"What am I doing?" she asked softly, more to herself than to him.

He slanted a glance in her direction as he left the town of Mount Henry and turned onto the turnpike. "You're taking the weekend off, that's all. And it's about time after you've worked so hard. I've got the skis and the room and you've got the time, for once. There's no sap to collect, is there, nothing to plant this time of year and nothing to harvest?"

"No," she agreed. "But..." She hesitated. How was she to explain that she didn't want to go through the cycle of loving and losing again? Wait a minute, she told herself. Who said anything about love? Certainly not her. And how could she lose somebody she never had? Maybe this was what she needed, a weekend with Max on neutral ground, not his weather station or her farm. That way when it ended there'd be nothing to remind her of him, not the horses or the close confines of the sugar shack or the hearth in her living room. Yes, this weekend she'd see that he was just another man, an ordinary man who could teach her to ski, but not take over her everyday life as he'd done before. Then at the end of the weekend she'd walk away knowing that it was nothing special, just a weekend off, and she was no one special, just a last-minute replacement. He was looking at her, waiting for her to finish her sentence.

"Nothing," she said. "You're right."

As they drove through the snowy foothills, Max asked Miranda about the syrup and she had to admit that she hadn't made as much money as she'd hoped.

"It's the middleman," she explained. "I sell to Green Mountain Merchants and they repackage my syrup into cute little jars with checkered gingham covers and sell it in the retail store for twice what I make because I don't have a store or a customer base to sell direct."

"What if you had a store, do you have anything else to sell?" he asked.

"Some apples. Grandma made wonderful apple butter, but that was a long time ago. The trees just don't produce the way they used to. I ought to prune them, but I don't know how. I have to face it, I need Green Mountain Merchants, but sometimes I wonder if it's worth it. All that work we did for so little money. Which should be half yours, by the way."

Max's headlights illuminated the narrow country road ahead. "I don't want any money. I did it for fun." He gave her a swift glance. It was dark now, so dark he couldn't make out her expression. He could only see the soft curve of her cheek and the faint outline of her breast under the soft camel-colored sweater with the little buttons up the front. He'd almost forgotten how the smell of her skin and her hair could take his breath away and make it impossible for him to speak. He didn't know what to say anyway, or he couldn't say what he wanted to say. That she'd been on his mind constantly these past weeks.

That he'd picked up the phone a dozen times to call her under the pretense of ordering something, but that he'd put it down again, knowing he couldn't hear her voice without unleashing the floodgates to his memory. That without half trying he could conjure up pictures of her riding Gretel bareback, her blond hair blowing in the wind behind her, her cheeks the color of her bright red jacket, her eyes laughing at him plodding along behind her.

He didn't need to hear her voice on the phone to remind him how she looked sitting next to him on that lumpy couch in the evening, half asleep, her head so close to his shoulder he could reach out and pull her to him. But he never had. He couldn't have done that to her or to himself. Because if he had, he wouldn't have stopped there; he would have kissed her until he couldn't stop and they'd passed the point of no return. And there they'd have been in the morning, tangled in each other's arms, sated, fulfilled and full of remorse. Because she trusted him and they both knew this relationship was destined to go nowhere.

If she hadn't found his boots, he'd be by himself now, headed for Cranmore. Instead, miracle of miracles, she was here beside him, one more time, one last time and then it was goodbye. If he needed to be reminded of what would happen if he considered falling in love again, he had only to think of Jack. He didn't feel sorry for him, he envied him. He had someone who cared about him enough to want him to come home. But how long would it last, a half-time marriage? Max's had lasted two years.

"Is that why you got divorced?" Miranda asked quietly as if she'd read his mind.

"What?" he asked startled.

"Your wife wouldn't let you go skiing?"

He shook his head. "Toward the end she didn't care where I went as long as I didn't come home." He turned the car into a driveway under the sign, Nordic Ski Area. "It wasn't her fault she couldn't deal with my schedule."

Miranda's eyes followed the signs that pointed to the ski lodge. "You mean she didn't know you'd be away so much?"

"She knew, but experiencing it is a different matter. Things happen, things come up, and I wasn't there. I don't blame her for finding someone else who'd be around all the time. I don't blame him, either, even though he was my best friend."

"Oh, Max." She reached for his arm and rested her hand on his shoulder.

"Don't feel sorry for me. It was my fault. Everyone agreed on that. Her parents, my parents. They wanted me to get another job. So I did. I got this job, the same kind as before, but as far away as possible. I had to make a choice, my wife or my job. I chose my job. That's the kind of guy I am." He felt Miranda's hand slide away from his shoulder.

"Well, here we are," he said, pulling up in front of a rambling stone lodge.

The lobby was flanked by an enormous stone fireplace with a fire burning brightly to welcome them. People in sleek après-ski outfits were sitting around the fire. The smell of hot mulled wine filled the air. Max sniffed hungrily and asked the desk clerk if they were too late for dinner.

After being assured they served until nine, Max carried his bag to his room, which adjoined hers. When he saw the connecting door between them, he felt a momentary panic. He wasn't made of New Hampshire granite. There was just so much temptation he could take.

Their eyes met and then looked away, she at the overhead light from the ceiling, he at the key in his hand. "See you in, what, a half hour or fifteen minutes?" he asked.

She nodded, went into her room and closed the door behind her. She turned on the hot water and sat on the edge of the tub, inhaling the steam and trying not to think too much about Max and his ex-wife and his feelings about marriage. For the moment she would concentrate on washing her hair and body even though she didn't have a change of clothes. What she would do without ski clothes she didn't know. She'd worry about that tomorrow.

Fortunately the management provided fluffy terry-cloth robes for the guests, which she was wearing when Max tapped on the door between their rooms. She leaned against the connecting door, pressing her forehead against the rich-smelling cedar wood. "I'm not ready," she said.

"When will you be ready?" he asked, his mouth only inches from hers on the other side of the door.

Her knees weakened by just the sound of his voice. Heaven help her, what was going to happen when they met face-to-face? She assured him she'd be ready in a few minutes, brushed her hair dry until it shone and buttoned up her sweater. When she opened the connecting door his hands were braced against the frame, his wide shoulders filling the doorway.

His eyes glittered like snow in the sunshine and he grinned at her as lightheartedly as if they'd never discussed his failed marriage. There was no trace of regret or sadness on his face. She smiled back.

"Where have you been?" he demanded. "Aren't you hungry? Weren't you worried about me starving to death over here?" Before she could answer he took her by the hand, through his room and out the door into the hall, down the stairs and into the dining room. There were several other tables still occupied, the lights were dim and there were candles and fresh flowers on each table. She looked around and breathed a sigh of pleasure. She'd never been to a ski lodge. She thought they'd be more rustic, less elegant. Skiing was not for Vermont farm girls who worked in complaint departments just to pay their taxes. But that didn't mean she couldn't appreciate the amenities, like the hand-woven carpets underfoot and the soft classical music in the background.

The dining room served a prix-fixe meal, which spared her the ordeal of trying to decide what to order. The first course was a thin sliver of prosciutto draped over a slice of melon, then a flavorful puree of vegetable soup lightly scented with fresh herbs. The main course was rare roast lamb studded with garlic cloves.

After she whisked the last bite off her plate, she paused and looked up at him. "I don't really belong here, you know."

"Because you're taking Jack's place?"

"Because everyone here is from New York. Didn't you see them in the lobby? They're the kind of people who order silk turtlenecks and lycra jumpsuits from Green Mountain to the tune of hundreds of dollars, just for one weekend."

Max lifted his wineglass and gave her a penetrating look. "Tell me about New York. What happened?"

"I told you. Everything and nothing. I was mugged, burglarized and harassed. And I got fired from my job."

"Why?"

"Because I wouldn't go out with the boss."

"Wait a minute. They can't do that. You could have filed a lawsuit."

"I know, but I didn't have the stomach for it, or the money. It was easier to just quit and come home. I told myself I'd never work for anyone again. If you work for yourself you can't be fired. I didn't know how hard it would be to make the farm pay for itself. So here I am working for somebody again." She folded her napkin in her lap and watched the waiter pour steaming coffee into her cup. "And no closer to being self-sufficient."

"Maybe you ought to diversify," he suggested.

"I know I should. In fact, I've always wanted to have a Christmas-tree farm on the back forty. You can buy seedlings from the forestry service for a few pennies apiece, but there's the question of selling the trees once they've grown. I don't know. Maybe I ought to sell the farm. Both Howard and Mr. Northwood have asked me if I was interested."

"Are you?"

"Not really. What would I do? Where would I go?"

The candlelight flickered in Max's eyes. He leaned forward as if he was going to suggest something. But there was nothing to say. She already knew the answer to her question. She had nothing else to do and no place to go.

"I'd hate to see you sell the farm," he said, a frown creasing his forehead.

"I won't. Not yet. Maybe I'll get those seedlings and put them in this spring."

"I'll drink to that," he said, raising his glass.

Miranda lifted her glass. She hoped he didn't think she expected him to help her. "That was a wonderful dinner," she said, draining the last of the wine in her glass. The last thing she wanted was for him to think she took him for granted.

"I see there's a moonlight sleigh ride at ten," he said, standing and following her out of the dining room.

Miranda pictured sleigh bells ringing, horses hooves clumping through the snow and she and Max together under a blanket in back. Which was not a good way to spend the evening. Not if she wanted to hold onto her vow not to get physically close to him. "I think I'll go to bed early," she said at the door to the lobby. "And try to get myself psyched up for skiing tomorrow."

"Sleighing isn't that strenuous," he said, his hand resting lightly on her shoulder. He ran his fingers across the soft wool of her sweater. "In fact it's a good place to get yourself psyched up for all kinds of activities."

His fingers burned a trail across her shoulder blades. Caught by the look in his eyes that kindled fires somewhere deep within her, she stood there wondering if he meant what she thought he meant. If he did she had to get back to her room immediately. She shouldn't have come. It was complete idiocy to go anywhere with this man. He wanted her, yes. She wanted him, too. But he'd made himself clear. He'd told her he'd chosen job over wife. No regrets. And he'd do it again. He didn't need to tell her that. She wasn't stupid. She could read between the lines.

"You go ahead, take a sleigh ride," she said.

The lines on his forehead deepened and he wrapped his arm around her shoulder. "Not without you. I'll walk you back to the room."

At her door he leaned forward, but before he could kiss her, she slipped under his arm and used her key to unlock the door.

"Good night," she said without looking at him, and carefully closed the door behind her. She pressed her ear against the door but heard nothing, no footsteps, nothing. Was he standing there, still leaning forward, puzzled by her abrupt departure? If so, it was time he got used to it. There would be no more kisses, no more searing looks that said more than words how much he wanted her and she wanted him.

She took off her clothes and slipped back into the soft terry-cloth robe. She'd almost forgotten the purpose of this trip. And that was to meet on neutral ground, to have the weekend free of emotional undercurrents. But it seemed they'd brought all their emotional baggage along with them. He and his failed marriage, she and her failed attempts to live an independent life.

She opened the French doors to the balcony, stepped outside in her bare feet and inhaled the clear cold air. On the balcony next to hers, only a few feet away, was the outline of a man, a man with a thick sweater that outlined his wide shoulders and broad chest, a man she couldn't stop thinking about.

"I thought you were going to bed early," he said, his voice as deep as the snow that drifted against the building.

"I am, as soon as I get some fresh air. What about you? What are you doing out here?"

"Same thing. Fresh air helps me think."

She couldn't help herself. She had to ask. "What about?"

He turned to face her, bracing his hands on the wooden railing and looking at her. "I'm thinking about you, dammit. I can't stop thinking about you. I've been thinking about you since I saw your picture in the catalog. Tell me I'm crazy, tell me you don't feel the same way and I'll go quietly, now before I make an ass of myself."

She wrapped her arms around her waist to keep from trembling, and it wasn't from the cold. "I don't feel anything," she said. "Can't we just be friends? Can't we go skiing together and enjoy the weekend? Then we'll say goodbye before it's too late."

"Too late for what?" he demanded.

"Before we . . . before we . . ." Her mind had shut down, her reasoning powers lost. She was blabbering. He stretched one leg over the railing and jumped over to land next to her. He gripped her shoulders tightly.

"Tell me again you don't feel anything. Go ahead."

She closed her eyes and held him to her, his sweater pressed to the white terry cloth that covered her breasts. Her arms tightened around his chest. "I don't. . .I can't. . .I lied, Max . . . please."

His lips were all over her face, kissing her lips, her cheeks, her eyelids. "Please what?" he muttered in her ear.

"Please don't do this," she pleaded. "It isn't right, you and me. It won't work."

He pulled back and stared at her, his mouth twisted in pain. He was breathing hard. "All right, you win. We'll go skiing. We'll enjoy the weekend. That's all. Is that what you want?"

She nodded helplessly and watched him vault back to his balcony. "It's not what I want," she said softly to herself. "It's what has to be."

The next day was so cold and so clear and so bright only a churl would have spoiled it by talking about anything more serious than the airy lightness of the crullers at breakfast or the depth of the snow or the quiet beauty of the untouched landscape. And neither Max nor Miranda had any desire to spoil their last whole day together.

He showed her how to take long gliding steps in her borrowed skis on the groomed trails and then they branched out into the deep thick powder where there were no trails and no people, just silence broken only by the sound of their skis cutting into the snow.

"I'll never forget," Miranda said, striding alongside of him, "when you threw that snowball at me at my party."

He grinned at her, his eyes skimming over the lined bib overalls he'd loaned her that bunched up at her ankles.

"Pretty good aim for a guy who grew up without benefit of snow."

"You mean you were aiming at me?" she asked indignantly.

"Of course not."

"I hadn't gotten over my surprise at seeing you there and then you hit me right in the shoulder. Why did you come, anyway? I had you pegged as a loner."

"I was. I still am. But your sister is very persuasive."

She slowed her pace. "Tell me about it."

"Does she know you're here this weekend?"

Miranda grimaced. "Not yet, but she'll find out. She'll probably be camped out on my doorstep waiting for me to come home."

"She called me the other day."

Miranda skidded into the dead branch of a fallen tree and her skis crossed at the tips. "What?"

"I had told the boys they should come up to see the weather station when we met that night, and she wanted to know when it would be convenient."

Miranda leaned over to untangle her skis and the blood rushed to her head. Ariel making plans behind her back. Ariel on the move again. She suspected her call had nothing to do with the boys visiting a weather station and everything to do with her preoccupation with Miranda's social life. "When are they coming?" she asked as casually as she could.

"Next Saturday."

"How nice." Briskly she brushed the snow from her gloves.

"They seem like good kids," he said, leaning forward on his ski poles.

"As long as they're not trying to attack each other. Keep your utensils under lock and key."

"I thought it was only snowballs they threw at each other."

"Oh, no, sticks and stones and old golf balls. Anything they can get their hands on."

"While we were outside they asked a lot of questions about my job."

"But who asked if they could come up and visit you, the boys or my sister?"

Max took his hat off and stuffed it into his pocket. Miranda watched the sun, now directly overhead, pick up the gold glints in his hair. "I'm not sure," he said.

"I'm pretty sure it wasn't the boys," Miranda said. "And I can tell you exactly what she's going to do next."

"What?" Max shaded his eyes against the sun.

"Come next Saturday or shortly before she'll call me and say that something's come up and she can't go to Mount Henry after all, but the boys are so looking forward to it and counting on it, could I possibly take them?"

"And what will you say?" Max asked, taking his sunglasses out of his pocket.

"I'll say no."

"Because you don't want to be manipulated or what?"

Impatiently she brushed the snow off the sleeves of her jacket. "You know why. We discussed this last night. After this weekend we're not going to see each other again. I thought we'd agreed."

"I didn't agree," he said, his lower lip jutting out stubbornly.

"You agree that you've got a job that takes precedence over anything else, don't you? And you agree that I've got no end of financial problems I have to solve."

"If you say so."

"I do say so and that's why I'm going to tell her to stop meddling in my life, once and for all." Miranda's voice had risen. Without knowing it she'd worked herself into a frenzy.

Max pushed his sunglasses up his nose. Then he reached over and gently brushed off the snow that dusted the top of her head. "Lunchtime," he announced. "Let's go back to the lodge."

She nodded, feeling foolish for going off on a tangent that way. She hoped it was the last time they'd ever have to talk about the situation. It was awkward and it was painful, for both of them.

In the afternoon they bundled into their terry-cloth robes and made their way to the spa behind the hotel, dramatically situated so that the hot steam rose against the snowbanks. Max had brought his swimming suit and Miranda had borrowed a one-piece maillot from the hotel. Max watched her slip into the tiled hot tub, the maillot clinging to her as if it were a second skin. He forced himself to look at the sky and analyze the structure of the altocumulus clouds overhead. Then he reached for the knob to activate the jets that sent the water bubbling against their tired back muscles.

By tilting his head back, he could look at the mountains in the distance, anywhere but at her smooth shoulders and the deep V of the swimsuit where it plunged between her breasts. He'd thought the spa would be relaxing, but instead it was stimulating—much too stimulating for him.

They could have gone back on the trail, but she'd been dragging her feet before lunch, and he'd thought this would be good for her. Good for her, maybe, but not for him. He watched her rest her head on the tiles and close her eyes. Her legs were stretched out in front of her, so close he could reach out and massage her tired feet if she wanted him to. He wasn't sure what she wanted. He heard what she said, but her eyes told him something else.

She was right about one thing. He had a job that was not compatible with any kind of serious entanglement. But he'd thought that maybe they could have a casual relationship, seeing each other on occasional weekends, like this. He let his gaze wander back in her direction, watching the way the water lapped at her breasts, knowing that there was nothing casual in the way he felt about her. And to be fair to her, he had to let it end this weekend.

He could do it, he thought, stretching his arms along the smooth tiles that edged the tub. He'd done it before, gone back to the mountain and buried himself in his work, and he could do it again. Only this time he'd just have a few more memories to push to the bottom of his subconscious. The picture of her sipping wine by candlelight and skiing through crisp new snow under the dazzling sun and now stretched out in front of him as if she were his and only his. By narrowing his eyes he could imagine her without the maillot, lying there just as she was, waiting... Oh Lord, what had he agreed to? What had he done?

The rest of the weekend passed in a blur of more images, each one etched in his memory whether he wanted them there or not. They went on the sleigh ride Saturday night. They took turns sitting next to the driver to avoid sitting next to each other, but on the way home somehow they ended up under the blanket in the back, her head on his shoulder, her silky hair against his cheek, so warm, so comfortable, so right together that it took forever to disentangle themselves when the sleigh stopped in front of the lodge. The horse puffed and snorted and the driver craned his neck to see if they'd fallen asleep.

Max got out first, held his arms out and she jumped into them. It wasn't easy standing there, under the lights from the hotel, aching to hold her to him, to feel the soft curves of her body mesh with the hard planes of his, but he dropped his arms and they walked slowly back to their rooms, and said good-night in the hall.

Before brunch on Sunday they donned snowshoes and went for a walk through the snow-covered fir trees. Miranda ducked under a low-hanging branch and caught up with Max. "This is so beautiful. I'm sorry your friend didn't get to come this weekend."

"I'm not," Max said, kicking clumps of snow out of his snowshoe. "I'm glad you came."

Miranda rubbed her hands together. "I am, too. I've had a wonderful time. I haven't had so much fun in the snow since I was a kid and we used to make angels in the snow."

"How do you make angels?"

She unstrapped her snowshoes and flopped down on her back in a patch of fresh snow. Then she moved her arms and legs back and forth in the snow, making wide indentations. She got to her feet to admire the form of an angel. "See?"

What he saw was her blond hair making a halo around her head. He turned her around gently by the shoulders and began to brush the snow off her jacket and her pants.

His hands lingered, his touch became more of a caress than he'd intended. She looked like an angel but she felt like a woman, warm, soft and responsive. She turned slowly to face him and he waited for her rebuke, but none came. She just stared at him for a long moment, her dark eyes reflecting the dazzling sun and the snow. Then, without speaking, she bent over and put her snowshoes back on, hiding her face from him and the sun.

After brunch they headed back to Mount Henry, where she got into her truck and after several tries started the engine. He stood in the parking lot long after she'd driven away, until the cold crept into his bones and he wondered if he'd ever be warm again. He knew he'd never be happy again. Not without Miranda. But that was how it had to be.

Chapter Seven

Ariel wasn't sitting on Miranda's front porch waiting for her. The house stood alone and forlorn under a dull, darkening sky. From brilliant sun and blue skies Miranda had come home to a run-down farmhouse in a sea of mud. To take the chill off the air inside she turned on the gas heater in the living room and changed into sweatpants and a sweatshirt she'd bought at the year-end closeout of discontinued items last season. Then she called her sister.

"Where have you been?" Ariel demanded just as Miranda knew she would. "I've been trying to call you all weekend."

"Skiing in New Hampshire."

"I don't believe it. You don't know how to ski."

Miranda propped her stocking-clad feet on the kitchen table. "I do now."

"Who taught you?"

"Max."

"Aha."

"Don't get excited. We had a nice time, but that's it. Then we said goodbye. For good. So don't get any ideas about throwing us together again. It's over, finished and done."

"Why?"

"Max loves his job. Period. There's no room in his life for anything or anyone else."

"How do you know?"

"He told me. Not in so many words, but I got the message. And I'm passing the message on to you. Now will you stop?"

"Of course." Miranda recognized the same patient tone of voice her sister used when her boys were out of control, and she gritted her teeth. "I have some good news for you," Ariel continued, changing the subject effortlessly. "Mr. Northwood told me he wants to make you an offer on the farm."

"I already know that."

"Not just an offer, a very generous offer. And I think you ought to listen to him this time."

Miranda looked around the kitchen at the cracked linoleum and the old canisters on the drainboard containing flour, sugar and oatmeal. "Doesn't the farm mean anything to you? Don't you care about your horses?"

"Of course I do," Ariel answered, "but I'm thinking of you and what's going to become of you stuck out there, pouring your money into a losing proposition. If you sold you could move to town and lead a normal life, have a normal *social* life."

"I wonder what that is," Miranda mused.

"See, you don't even know. Just tell me you'll listen to what Northwood has to say."

"All right."

After she hung up Miranda realized neither of them had mentioned Ariel's trip to Mount Henry with the boys. Now that Ariel knew there was no hope in getting Max and Miranda together, maybe she'd cancel it. In any case it was no concern of Miranda's whether they went or not.

She picked her way through the mud to feed the horses and wondered what it would be like to live in a tidy little house in town with a sidewalk out in front. She'd never be late to work because it would be just a short walk away. And on Tuesday nights she could play Bingo at the Elks Hall. She shuddered. Was that what Ariel meant by a normal social life? Restlessly she walked around the field in her rubber boots as night fell around her. In her mind she saw acres of fir trees, full and bushy, ready for harvest. Then she thought of planting the seedlings, one by one, and years later trucking them to a lot somewhere to sell. And she knew she couldn't do it, not alone.

The next day at work Mr. Northwood called her into his office and just as Ariel had predicted, made her a generous offer for the farm.

"May I ask why you want the old place?" Miranda asked, standing in front of his desk, looking down at the old man in his flannel shirt and twill crew pants. She wondered if he'd stick to his story of wanting "a little place in the country."

"Just good business, Miranda. We get our syrup from you, all you can harvest. If we own the farm, we can eliminate the middleperson—you."

"I see," she said, but she didn't. It was such a small amount of syrup she produced that the Northwoods had to buy from farms all over the state to supply their customers. Why not buy up somebody else's farm? She told him she'd have to think about it and went back to her cubicle.

At least it gave her something to think about besides Max. It was after work when thoughts of him came creeping back, making her feel restless, depressed and at loose ends. She should prune the apple trees, start on the Christmas tree project or buy a pair of goats and breed them, but what was the use if she wasn't going to stay?

She couldn't bring goats with her to town. She couldn't bring the horses, either, they'd have to be boarded somewhere. These were only some of her worries, all of which were more important than never seeing Max again. Then why did she continue to think about him? Habit, just a bad habit she'd have to break.

The next day Ariel invited her to dinner. Rob had been hunting and she was cooking a roast duck. "One of Rob's hunting buddies will be here, too," she said.

Miranda felt a sinking sensation in the pit of her stomach. "How nice."

"He is nice," Ariel said defensively. "He's not married, never has been and he has no hang-ups about his job being so all-important."

"What is his job?" Miranda asked politely, propping her elbows on the counter in the retail store where Ariel was arranging sweaters in an attractive display.

"He's a taxidermist," Ariel said, fixing her sister with a challenging gaze.

Miranda swallowed hard to keep from saying anything critical. "What can I bring?"

"Just a positive attitude," Ariel said, giving the last sweater a pat on the shoulder pad.

To Miranda's surprise Rob's friend was very nice, very nice and thirty pounds overweight. He and Rob talked about what a good hunting season it was. They asked Miranda about her experience cross-country skiing and she was able to describe it without mentioning Max at all. In fact, listening to her tell about it, one might have thought she had gone all by herself. Only Ariel knew what she was leaving out, and Miranda could tell by the gleam in her eye, that she was dying to know. The dinner party was a success and the subject of taxidermy never came up.

With Max the subject of weather or mountains always came up. His love of the outdoors and the challenge of his job was a part of him, so deeply ingrained she couldn't imagine him without it. She wished she felt the same way about the farm. Did she really belong there? Could she ever make it pay? Would she miss it if she left?

Before she left Ariel's, Miranda went upstairs to say good-night to the boys. "How's school?" she asked, leaning against the ladder that connected the bunk beds in Scott's room.

Scott looked down at her from the top bunk and wrinkled his nose. "Miss Wilson is mean."

"Miss Wilson, is she still there?"

"Yeah, and she remembers you, Aunt Miranda. She says you were her best student."

"She taught me everything I know."

"You know that guy who we were having that snowball fight with at your party?" Brian asked from the doorway.

Miranda turned around. "Max? Yes, I know him."

"We're going up to his mountain to see him on Saturday. We might get snowed in like you did. Then we wouldn't have to go to school anymore."

"So that's why you're going."

"Naaa. He's got more snow up there than we've ever seen in our lives. Jillions of feet. We're taking our sleds."

"Also," Scott added, "it's the home of the world's worst weather. The worst."

"Uh-huh. That's what I heard. Well, have a good time, if you get snowed in and I don't see you again."

She thanked her sister for the dinner and drove home to the empty farmhouse. Why it seemed emptier than ever these days she didn't know. She knew she had to make a decision soon, but she could barely decide what to wear to work in the morning let alone a decision that would affect the rest of her life.

The week dragged by and Ariel never mentioned going up to Mount Henry. Not that it was any concern of Miranda's what her sister did on the weekend. It was just that she'd expected her to pull some sort of stunt. Here it was Friday noon and she still hadn't said anything. Miranda was lunching with the girls as usual at the steak house, discussing the latest gossip in town about the sheriff and the church organist and the Northwoods' latest scheme to cut expenses. Finally they turned to Miranda.

"How's that guy that stayed at your house bottling syrup?" Mavis asked.

"Fine, but he's gone now. Gone for good."

"I don't get it, I thought he was someone special." She licked her lips.

"He was just a customer with a complaint, that's all. I had to follow up on him until he got everything he wanted."

Mavis giggled. "You mean he finally got everything he wanted?"

Miranda blushed as her friends around the table erupted into laughter. "Look," she said, "the man lives in another state and he's married to his job. So there's no point in discussing him any further."

"Are you sure?" Donna asked. "Because I heard that Ariel's going up there this weekend to fix things up."

Miranda dropped her fork with a clatter. "What?"

Donna clapped her hand over her mouth.

"Time to go," Lianne announced abruptly, putting a ten-dollar bill on the table.

Miranda told herself they couldn't be serious. They were just trying to get a rise out of her. On the other hand, knowing her sister...

On Friday evening when the phone rang she knew it would be Ariel, but it was Howard telling her he'd match any offer by Mr. Northwood. "It must get lonely there all by yourself," he noted.

She would never admit it, to Howard or to anyone else, but it *was* lonely. For the first time in her life she felt it, a bone-chilling loneliness that got worse every day. No one called and she called no one all weekend. She didn't listen to the radio because she didn't want to hear the weather report. More than once she pictured the boys sledding on Mount Henry, making snowmen or angels in the snow. And she imagined Ariel sitting in the weather station having coffee, talking to Max. About what? The weather? Her? For once she was glad to go back to work on Monday.

But Ariel didn't come to work on Monday. They said she'd called in sick, but Miranda wondered if she was snowed in on Mount Henry. The thought sent a spear of envy through her. Snowbound with Max, alone on top of the world. The memories came flooding back. The snow in his hair, holding the underwear up to see if it fit, sharing the view of the mountains at daybreak.

At lunchtime she walked to Ariel's house and knocked on the front door. Ariel came to the door and opened it just a crack. "Have you had chicken pox?" she asked.

"Of course I have. We had it at the same time, don't you remember?"

"Then come in."

Miranda walked into the living room and stepped over a vacuum cleaner. "What's wrong, who's got chicken pox?"

Ariel ran her hand through her hair distractedly. "Scott does and Brian will probably be next. So I'll be out of work for a couple of weeks. I don't know what old man North-wood's going to say about that."

"You'll use up all your sick leave for the next two years."

Ariel shrugged. "That's the breaks."

Miranda perched on the edge of the couch. "When did this happen?"

"He started itching and scratching yesterday when we got back from the mountain. This morning he woke up with little red dots all over his stomach. That's when I realized what it was. And three other kids in his class have it. It's very contagious."

Scott's mournful voice floated downstairs and Miranda and Ariel went up to take him a glass of apple juice. His little speckled face was flushed and Miranda sat on the edge of the bottom bunk bed to talk to him.

"Did you see any of the world's worst weather while you were on the mountain?" she asked, taking the cold compress from Ariel and holding it against his forehead.

"Nope, but it's a cool place where Max works."

"How'd you get up there?"

"We got a ride in a big snow machine from a guy, then he came back and picked us up. He said when the snow melts we can bring the whole class on a field trip."

Miranda took the compress off his head and looked at Ariel. They left Scott with a new comic book and went back downstairs.

"Max was great with the kids," Ariel remarked. "He said he's always wanted some of his own."

Miranda looked out the front window. "Where would he keep them, in the storage shed?"

Ariel sank into the easy chair. "Come on, Miranda, he must live somewhere. He can't just stay at the weather station all the time."

"I guess he has an apartment somewhere." Miranda swallowed her pride and asked her sister if he'd said anything else besides that he wanted to have children.

"He asked about you."

Miranda's heart fluttered, impossibly, unreasonably, encouraged.

"I told him you were pining away," Ariel said.

"You didn't."

"No, I said you were fine, but are you?"

"Of course, why?"

"Because you look peaked, as Grandma would say. Have you been eating your oatmeal in the morning?" Ariel asked.

Miranda dismissed her concern with a wave of her hand. "Physically I'm fine. I just don't know what to do next. I can't bring myself to sell the farm. It's too much a part of me, of our family." She brushed back a wisp of hair that had escaped from her French braid.

Ariel nodded understandingly and Scott called again from upstairs.

Miranda went to the door. "I have to get back to work."

"Thanks for coming. Has Max had chicken pox?"

"I have no idea. Why?"

"Adults can get it if they haven't had it as a child, but if they do it can be serious. I'd better call and warn him, unless you..." Ariel's voice trailed off. She had circles under her eyes as if she'd been up all night with Scott.

"All right, I'll call him," Miranda said.

When she returned to work she buried herself behind the walls of her cubbyhole to muffle her voice from her colleagues and dialed the number of the weather station.

The sound of his deep voice tinged with his Southern accent sent shivers up her spine. Her throat tightened and she couldn't speak. She thought of hanging up and making Ariel call. It was her fault he'd been exposed to chicken pox.

"Hello," he said. "Anyone there?"

"It's me," she said finally. "Miranda."

"Miranda," he said. "Are you all right?"

"I'm fine, but you've been exposed to chicken pox." There, she'd said it. Now she could hang up. But she didn't. "One of my nephews just came down with it."

"Don't worry, I never catch anything."

"Well, I just wanted to warn you."

"Thanks, but I'm fine."

"The incubation period is two weeks."

"I'll remember that." There was an awkward silence. Then he said, "Your sister tells me you're seeing some taxidermist."

"What?" She shot up straight in her seat, forgetting her friends might hear her, forgetting everything but her indignation. "I saw him once...at her house. How could she?"

If Ariel had been there she would have choked her. "I'd hardly call that seeing someone," she blurted.

"Oh." There was relief in that one drawn-out word, relief and hope and maybe even a smile. For a brief moment Miranda basked in that smile as if it were a ray of sunshine on a gloomy March day. Then she came to her senses. "Good luck," she said. "I hope you don't catch the chicken pox."

"Thanks."

Max had no idea what chicken pox felt like, but he was pretty sure he didn't have it. He didn't have chicken pox, but he had something else. A mysterious disease that took the joy out of his life, that caused him to stare out into space without seeing the magnificent mountains or the reflection of the sunrise over the ocean. A strange malady that caused him to live in the past, back to the weekend he'd spent with Miranda.

He wondered what would have happened if he hadn't leveled with her about his failed marriage, about his decision to chuck it all and bury himself in his work. Would he still be sitting here staring into an empty future? He told himself it wasn't empty, that it was full of promise and opportunity for someone who could devote himself to it without distractions. He was always available to work an extra shift or put in extra hours. He had enough seniority that they'd never transfer him to an office. He could look forward to years of facing the world's worst weather. Alone.

He thought he'd gotten over her. Then her sister had told him she was seeing someone special and it had hit him, knocked the breath out of him as if he'd been caught in a two-hundred mile-per-hour wind. Now that he knew it wasn't true, he ought to feel better, but hearing her voice had made him feel worse. Made him want to see her, hold her, kiss her again. It was irrational. It was worse than that;

it was irresponsible. He'd tried it and it hadn't worked. It wasn't fair to anyone to try again.

And so it went. Two weeks of arguing with himself. One week on and one week off. When he came back to the weather station he felt as if he'd been worked over in a prize fight with every muscle aching. When in reality he'd only been beating up on himself. Even Jake noticed.

"What did you do this week, run into a hurricane?" Jake asked from the front seat of the Sno-Cat.

"You're close," Max admitted, squinting into the bright sun. His eyes stung, and his head pounded even though he was used to the sun and accustomed to the altitude. "Anything I should know about?"

"One hundred percent sunshine, winds averaging twelve miles per hour. Not like any March I've ever seen." He shook his head. "I'd rather see some weather up here."

Max nodded. He'd rather see some weather, too. It would give him something to do, a reason to justify his existence, a way to keep his mind off Miranda. There was no challenge in reading instruments under a clear sky with no precipitation to measure. He went inside to escape the sunshine and to read the logs from the past week. But reading Jack's small print made his head hurt more and he lay down on the daybed in the corner, where he fell asleep in broad daylight.

The ringing of the telephone woke him up. He staggered to his feet, wondering where he was and how he got there. It was Ariel, Miranda's sister.

"It's been two weeks," she explained. "I hope you didn't get the chicken pox."

"No, no," he assured her, scratching his stomach through his polo shirt. "I'm just fine."

"That's good. I've been worried about you. So has Miranda."

He reached for the light switch above the desk. "Has she?" By now he should know to take everything Ariel said with a grain of salt, but it was possible, just possible, that Miranda might worry about him. On the other hand...

"Well, tell her I'm fine." He would be fine, too, as soon as his head stopped pounding and this rash on his stomach went away.

Ariel told him how much the boys appreciated their visit to the weather station and how one of them was back in school and the other one had just come down with chicken pox.

"What did you say the symptoms were?" Max asked.

"A fever and a red, itchy rash."

"On the stomach?"

"You mean you've got it? I knew it. I'm so sorry. It's all my fault. Don't move. Help is on the way."

"I don't need help," he assured her. "It's just a kid's disease."

"A kid's disease that's serious for adults."

"Not for me," he said, switching off the light and closing his eyes. "I'm okay."

Ariel caught Miranda on her way out of the building that Friday evening. She grabbed the raglan sleeve of Miranda's parka. "Stop. Max has chicken pox. You've got to get up there right away."

Miranda's eyes widened and her heart stopped beating for a second. "Why, what happened?"

"It's what could happen. In adults chicken pox can lead to pneumonia, and pneumonia can lead to death."

Miranda stared at her under the single light in the parking lot. "How do you know?"

"I called him," Ariel explained. "I knew he'd never say anything unless I pried it out of him. That's the way men are. But I can tell he's suffering. I'd go if I could, but I have Brian...."

Miranda ran her hand distractedly across the hood of her car. "I don't know anything about childhood diseases."

"Yes, you do. You were wonderful with Scott the other day. We can't stand here talking. Follow me to my house. I'll give you all the stuff you'll need and you can leave from there. And don't worry about the horses. I'll send Rob out there to feed them."

Her head spinning, Miranda followed her sister to her house. Scott, now recovered, was chasing the cat around the dining-room table. Brian was on the couch watching TV and Rob was in the garage. Upstairs in the bedroom, Ariel filled a tote bag with old towels to make compresses, aspirin and some long underwear. She added more clothes for Miranda and some lotion to relieve itching.

"Oh, and here's the *Doctor's Guide to Children's Health.*" Ariel held up a well-worn paperback book. "Don't lose it, I use it all the time."

"I can see that." Miranda turned the dog-eared pages to the section on chicken pox. She read the part about pneumonia leading to death and she slammed the book shut, dropped it into the canvas bag and said goodbye.

"I'll call that nice man who drives the tractor," Ariel said, following her sister down the stairs, "and tell him it's a medical emergency and ask him to meet you at the bottom of the mountain to give you a ride up." Before Miranda left she handed her a plastic container of her homemade beef barley soup.

Miranda nodded and got into her car. She wondered if Fred would really meet her in the Sno-Cat. Two hours and many miles later she saw he was waiting just where he had been the last time.

"Should I call a doctor?" he asked as she got into the Sno-Cat with her overflowing canvas bag.

"I don't know. I'll have to see how he is when I get up there."

"You a nurse?"

"Not really. I'm just a friend."

"Aren't you the lady with the boots?" He peered into her bag. "What'cha got this time?"

"A few first-aid items."

"Good. I didn't think he looked so good the last time I saw him."

"When was that?"

"About two weeks ago. I've been on paternity leave. He'd been skiing, but underneath the suntan, he looked peaked to me."

That made two of them, Miranda thought, anxiously clutching her sack. Did Max expect her? What if he didn't want her? What if he didn't want anybody? Maybe she should ask Fred to wait while she went in and asked. But when Fred stopped the Sno-Cat in front of the observatory, she jumped out of the Sno-Cat and never looked back. She pictured Max lying on his back unconscious, his long tall body covered with red spots. She scarcely heard Fred wish her good luck as he gunned the engine for the trip back down the mountain. Despite her heavy bag she took the steps to the heavy front door two at a time, and pounded against it with her fist. When he didn't answer she let herself in. The room was pitch-dark.

She stumbled across the floor and switched on the light above the desk. There in the corner on the daybed Max lay sleeping with one arm over his head as if to protect himself. She'd never seen him asleep before, never known him to look as vulnerable as he did now. Her heart turned over and her eyes smarted with tears. She crossed the room and stood by the side of his bed. His chin was grazed with the dark stubble of a beard, his forehead dotted with red spots. She wanted to lay her palm against his cheek and hold his hand. She wanted to put her arms around him and tell him everything was going to be all right. But was it?

Under her gaze he shifted to his side and opened his eyes just a crack. "Oh Lord," he muttered, "now I'm delirious."

"Max," she whispered, kneeling down next to his bed. "How are you?"

"Miranda?" he said, rubbing his eyes with his fist. "How did you get here?"

"In the Sno-Cat. We were worried. I heard...Ariel said... Are you all right?"

"Fine. Just tired. Tried to go out ... couldn't."

"No, no, you can't go out. Can't do anything. You might get pneumonia and ... and ..." She blinked back the tears that sprung to her eyes again. He wouldn't get pneumonia and he wouldn't die. She wouldn't let him. "You've got to rest."

He cracked a half smile. "I am resting."

Encouraged by his smile, she leaned forward on her knees and tilted her head to look into his eyes.

He held out his hand to stop her. "Don't get too close. You'll catch whatever I've got."

"Chicken pox. I've already had it."

"Well, in that case..." He reached for her hand and gripped it tightly. His fingers were strong but his palm was warm, too warm. He closed his eyes and pressed her hand to his cheek. "I don't understand how you got here, but I'm glad you came. Maybe you told me, but my brain's not working very well."

"I came to take care of you."

He shook his head slowly. "You can't do that. You've got the farm and the horses and your job."

"This is the weekend. I don't have anything else to do but take care of you."

"I don't want to be taken care of," he protested.

"You took care of me," she reminded him lightly, turning her hand in his to feel the calluses on his palm, reminding her of all the hard work he'd done for her. "Remember what you said, that if you were sick you'd let me put you to bed and even kiss you good-night."

There was no mistaking the smile that angled the corners of his mouth or the gleam in his half-closed eyes. "Anytime," he muttered. "Anytime."

Chapter Eight

Reluctantly Miranda eased her hand out of his and got up off the floor. If she could make him well by putting him to bed and kissing him good-night, she would, but first she had to bring down the fever and make him comfortable. She covered him with a blanket and went to put the soup on the stove and soak the towels in cold water. Then she sat by his bed in the same chair she'd fallen asleep in the last time she was there, holding a cold compress on his head while he drifted in and out of sleep. In her other hand she held the medical guide and read about chicken pox.

Sometimes he muttered something about the clouds and the precipitation or the wind speed. She brushed back the thick blond hair that stuck to his forehead and prayed that he only had chicken pox. What if she hadn't come? What if he'd been lying here alone and he got pneumonia? When he blinked his eyes she put her arm around him and helped him sit up.

"You're still here," he said, squinting at her with bleary eyes.

She nodded and handed him a glass of apple juice. Seeing him lying helpless almost made her forget how independent he usually was. As for her, she'd had enough independence for the moment. She was ready to admit she couldn't manage the farm by herself, but only to herself. She'd never admit it to Max or to her sister, they'd jump to conclusions. Independence was a quality she admired but hadn't quite achieved yet. If she were more independent she wouldn't feel this longing steal over her, this desire to be where he was, to share his thoughts, his hopes and his dreams.

She knew he wanted her. She saw the look in his eyes, felt the heat of his touch, but she also knew that his hopes and dreams didn't include her, no matter how much he desired her.

He set his glass down on the table next to the bed. "Tell me again why you're here and who you are."

Her eyes widened in alarm. "Max, don't you know?"

"Humor me. I want to touch you and hear you talk so I know I'm not dreaming."

She leaned back in her chair and gave in. The least you could do for an adult with chicken pox was to humor them. "Okay, I'm Miranda Morrison. I came to take care of you because you're sick, but normally I'm in customer service."

A crooked grin creased his face. "Some service."

She nodded and squeezed his hand. The current from his body flowed to hers and back again. They made a closed circuit. His fever was bringing back his Southern accent. She felt her defenses crumbling.

"Why is it the only time you and I are in the vicinity of a bed together one of us is too sick to do anything about it?" he asked.

"If we weren't, I'm afraid of what might happen. I'm afraid of what you do to me," she muttered under her breath.

"I haven't done anything yet," he said, turning on his side and holding her hand against his heart so she could hear it pound.

"That's what I'm afraid of," she said half to herself. She pulled her hand away and sat up straight in her chair, summoning her strength. "We've been through this before. And it always comes out the same way. There's an attraction between us. I feel it and you feel it. But I've got a farm to run that needs all my money and all my attention. You've got a job that requires half your time and all your interest. And that's why we only get together when one of us is sick, when one of us needs the other."

"What if I said I needed you all the time," he suggested, his eyes bright and feverish.

"You mean half the time."

He looked at her for a long moment, then he closed his eyes and for just a second she thought his lashes were wet, and she felt her heart contract. She looked again and saw she was mistaken. But she knew she'd hurt him, reminding him of his failed half-time marriage. She told herself it was better to remind him now than later.

She gave him beef barley soup for dinner. Then, sitting on the edge of his bed, she washed his face with a cool cloth, studying the character lines in his face, sliding the cloth under his chin behind his ears.

He looked at her, his blue eyes narrowed to slits. "What about the rest of me?" he asked. "I'm burning up."

She nodded, helping him pull his sweatshirt off over his head, revealing a smooth, well-toned chest. She took the thermometer from the bag Ariel had given her, shook it down and put it under his tongue. Then she took the cool, damp cloth and slowly worked her way from his shoulders to his waistband, where the rash disappeared. His gaze held hers, stronger than his grip on her hand had been, and she was unable to look away. She felt the texture of his skin and the tone of his muscles. The heat from his body seared her hand. Frightened, she took the thermometer out of his mouth, fearing the worst, but it read only one hundred degrees.

She eased his shirt back over his head, her hands lingering on his shoulders. "Good news," she said. "You're not on fire."

"You could have fooled me."

She cleared her throat. "I mean your temperature's almost normal. I don't think you've got pneumonia."

"Are you sure?" he asked. "I've got all the symptoms, chills, fever and a pain right here." He pointed to his heart. "You haven't even listened to my chest."

She leaned forward. She knew it was a trick. She knew it was a mistake, but she put her head against the soft gray of his sweatshirt and felt his arms go around her and hold her tight. She exhaled slowly, feeling the weight of her problems slide off her shoulders, feeling the warmth of his body creep into hers, hearing the steady heartbeat that matched her own. She felt so safe, so secure, that she fell asleep in the arms of the man she'd come to care for, who—for some reason—was always taking care of her.

For Max the dream and the reality of falling asleep with Miranda in his arms merged into one that night. It wasn't exactly as he'd dreamed it, but he reminded himself that one of them was sick, too sick to take advantage of the situation, and the other was too scared. Which was just as well, because in the morning one of them would regret it, maybe both of them. In the meantime he drifted in and out of sleep, inhaling the scent of her skin and her hair, feeling the weight of her body against his, knowing that it was only his sickness that kept her there and vowing to stay sick for as long as possible. Because it wasn't likely to happen again.

The next morning she was up and dressed before dawn as he knew she'd be. She cooked breakfast for him but wouldn't meet his gaze. He should have known. She reached for the empty breakfast tray on his lap and he reached for her arm. "Miranda, nothing happened."

"I slept with you. I came here to take care of you and I slept in your bed, on top of you."

"I'm sorry, I was too tired to stop you." She finally met his gaze, her eyes full of self-reproach. "Do you want to leave?" he asked. "I don't have pneumonia."

She frowned. "You still have chicken pox. What about your work, your observations? Maybe I can help." She gestured toward the computer on the desk and the telescope on the tripod in front of the window.

"Well, okay," he said reluctantly. "There's not much weather to observe today. I'll read the anemometer in here, but you can observe the sky cover and estimate visibility." He yawned in spite of himself. It made him tired just to think of it. How did kids ever survive this disease, anyway? Maybe chicken pox was more serious than he thought. It was certainly itchier. Just when he was rubbing ferociously against his stomach, Miranda came out with some soothing cream from the bottom of that seemingly bottomless tote bag.

She slipped her cool hand under his shirt and while she stopped the itching, she created other problems, which caused him to flop over on his stomach. That left her to work the magic cream into his shoulder blades and down his back. He moaned and her hands stilled.

"Is it that bad?" she asked softly.

"Terrible," he groaned.

"I'm sorry. Where does it hurt?"

"All over."

"What can I do?"

His answer was unintelligible.

She slid her hands out from under the shirt and covered him with the blanket. While he napped, she put on her jacket and went outside on the observation deck to inhale the crisp, clear air. She didn't know what the visibility was in miles, but she could see from the White Mountains to the glimmer of the ocean beyond. Directly below her in three feet of snow grew clumps of balsam fir, still dusted with white. Slate-colored junco birds shook the branches of the trees. She tilted her face to let the late winter sun warm her face. High, puffy clouds floated by. If this was the world's worst weather, then what was the best? The peace and the solitude seeped into her bones and she understood what he meant about the lure of the mountains.

When she came back in he was sitting up raking his hand through his hair. "Well," he said, "what's the visibility? I have to phone in my report in five minutes."

"I felt like I could see forever."

"Forever doesn't quite make it down in Portland. Was it seventy or eighty miles? Could you see Mount Killington or Adams?"

"I'm not sure," she admitted, giving him a sharp look. Was this the cranky stage she'd read about in the medical book?

"Never mind, what's the temperature?"

"Fifty-eight."

"Very good. Sky cover, clouds?"

"Yes."

"Altocumulus or altostratus?"

She shrugged her shoulders.

He staggered to the window and looked at the sky. "Altostratus at 8000 feet. Would you bring me the cordless phone?"

He gave his report from the edge of his bed in his wrinkled gray sweats, bare feet on the floor, gauging the wind speed by the sound it made against the window, giving an in-depth report, including the humidity. She watched him from the door of the kitchen where she was making tea, impressed by the complexity of the information and his mastery of it.

When he finished he set the phone on the floor and flung himself back into bed. "What's wrong with me?" he called to her. "One report and I'm wiped out. And I didn't even go out, you did."

She carried two cups of tea to the table next to his bed. "I'm afraid I wasn't much help."

He cocked his head to one side and looked at her. "For a rookie you weren't bad."

She sipped her tea. "Maybe I'll do better tomorrow."

He juggled his cup. "You're staying until tomorrow?"

"I don't want to leave until you're completely well. I never knew everything that went into your work. How did you get so good at it?"

"Experience. The first thing I learned was to trust my instruments. The second thing I learned was that if I couldn't trust my instruments, I had to trust my instincts."

She spooned a dollop of honey into her cup. "What do you mean?"

"Weather watching isn't a science and it isn't an art. It's somewhere in between. That's what I like about it."

"Is this what you always wanted to do?"

He shielded his eyes to look out the window. "Not really. I could have gone in several directions. But when I was a kid I kept a rain gauge, so maybe I was destined to end up like this. Who knows?"

She set her cup down. Who knew? She knew. It was destiny, and how could she fight destiny? He was meant to be where he was, and she was meant to be where she was. It was only an accident that they'd met at all.

She met his steady gaze over the top of his cup and the look in his eyes confused her. There was warmth in his blue eyes, warmth and gratitude and something else she couldn't decipher. She looked out the window. It was crazy coming up here again. There was something about the solitude that wove a spell around them, made her feel as if they were the only two people in the world. From every window was a spectacular view of sky and mountains. From every direction was wilderness. No people. Only them.

"This wasn't always a mountain," he said, following her gaze. "Three hundred million years ago it was a seabed with fish and other forms of life. That was before my time," he explained. "Then the earth was forced upward into these White Mountains you see around you. The one we're on is made up of the oldest material. Ancient mud turned into tough mica schist."

She turned her gaze from the spectacular peaks to look at him. "I thought it was granite."

"No granite in the Granite State's highest peak. When the snow melts, sometime this spring, you'll see the layers of rock along the trail, one for every glacier that passed through during the ice age, but no granite."

She didn't say that just as surely as the snow melted she, too, would be gone, never to return to this spectacular place. Never to see the layers of rock along the trail. He would be alone again, leading the life he wanted, the life destiny had chosen for him. Maybe he realized it, too, because he trailed off and just as suddenly as he'd begun his geology lecture, he stopped.

In the afternoon he napped again and she went outside to walk around the observatory, to pick up the dry snow in her hands and hear her boots crunch through it.

When Max woke up his mouth was dry, his head hurt and he wasn't sure where he was. One thing was sure, he was alone. She was gone. The emptiness in the room echoed from wall to wall. She'd promised to stay until tomorrow. What had made her leave? Something he'd said? Something he hadn't said?

What could he say, that he wanted her around all the time? What was the point if it was impossible? It would just make things worse. It was better to pretend that he was just what she thought he was, a loner, a man more comfortable with things than with people. It was true once. Only that was before he knew Miranda. Before she came into his life and turned it upside down. Maybe she thought it would work, a half-time relationship. But he knew better. He'd learned the hard way. And he'd never put anyone else through it. Especially someone he cared for as much as he cared for her.

She was everything he'd ever wanted and everything he couldn't have. She was light and warmth and as beautiful as a mountain sunrise, all pink and gold. He could talk to her or he could just sit next to her and not say a word. She made this sterile observation tower feel like a home in just the one day she'd been there. If she stayed any longer he might lose what willpower he had left. He might tell her... might ask her...

There were footsteps on the stairs and the heavy front door opened. She was back. Her face glowed, her gloves were caked with white powder. She gave him a smile as dazzling as the snow outside. He didn't know he'd been holding his breath, waiting, hoping....

"Where were you?" he growled. "I thought you'd left."

"Nope," she said, hanging her jacket on the coatrack next to the door. "You can't get rid of me yet. How do you feel?"

"Terrible."

"I'll make some toast."

"No more toast and no more tea. I want some bourbon from the cabinet up there." He pointed to the shelves above the desk. "And then I want something I can get my teeth into." He narrowed his eyes and gave her a long, hard, hungry look. If only he were well, if only he dared let her know how he felt. He wanted to get up, move around, take her in his arms, but he fell back weakly on the bed.

She reached for the bottle. "You seem better today." She poured a small amount into a shot glass and handed it to him. "Shall I look and see what's in your freezer?"

He gave her a puzzled look.

"To see if there's something you can sink your teeth into."

"Go ahead. Lord, I feel like I've been trapped inside this sick body for weeks."

"I'm sorry the boys did this to you. They should never have come up here. Look what happened."

"It wasn't their fault. They're a lot of fun. We had a good time."

"That's what they said."

He watched her cross the room to the kitchen, the soft lines of her wool slacks accentuating her slim hips and long legs. He heard her raise the lid of the large freezer.

"I was an only child. I hated it. If I were married I'd have a dozen kids," he said.

"Where would you put them?" Her voice floated out of the kitchen.

"That's the problem," he admitted, knotting the blanket in his hand and wishing he had another shot of bourbon. "They'd be down below and I'd be up here. That's no good. That's why I'm not married and instead of a dozen kids I've got a room full of instruments."

She poked her head around the kitchen door. The sympathy in her dark eyes was unmistakable even from across the room.

"Don't feel sorry for me. It's my choice."

"I know that." She held a package of meat in her hands. "What about steak?"

"What do you want?" he asked.

"Steak is fine with me."

He propped himself on one elbow. "I mean, what do you want, a dozen kids or what?"

She walked back into the room toward his bed, took his glass and refilled it for him. Then she poured one for herself. As if she were at home. As if she lived there, too. The thought warmed him as much as the bourbon did. She swirled the liquid in the glass. Then she sat down in the big wide armchair and looked out the window as the sunset cast an orange glow over the mountains.

"I don't know what I want," she said slowly. "I know what I don't want and that's to work for somebody else. But I'm beginning to think living off the farm is an impossible dream. I could sell it. Mr. Northwood made me a good offer the other day, but then where would I go, and what would I do? I've already tried the city and I've tried the country. I've failed at both."

"Don't say that." He hated to hear the discouragement in her voice. He set his glass down and sat up straight. There were small lines etched between her fine eyebrows. Her mouth was set in a straight line. "You've made the farm into a home, without using money or material things. By just being there, by caring about it. It's a warm place, a place where people feel comfortable."

"You like the farm?" she asked as dusk fell over the room.

"I love your farm. I don't want you to sell it." He locked his hands together. What was he saying? He had no right to advise her, to tell her what to do. "But you have to do what's right for you," he added.

"Yes, well..." She stood and went to the kitchen. "Time for dinner. How do you like your steak?"

They both liked their steak medium rare, smothered with peppers and onions and mushrooms, all of which were found in packages in the depths of his freezer. She made coffee after dinner and she sat in the chair next to him in the dark. He told her the light hurt his eyes, but the truth was it was easier to talk when she couldn't see his face, see the look in his eyes or suspect the depths of feeling that lurked in them and threatened to spill over.

"I appreciate your coming up here to take care of me," he said.

"It's nothing more than you did for me."

"I've been sick before, by myself. And I got well by myself."

"Are you trying to tell me you don't need me?" she asked. "I know that."

"I'm trying to tell you I've gotten used to having you around. I'm trying to tell you I'll miss you when you go. But I'm not doing a very good job of it."

"I understand," she said quietly. "I also understand how you feel about the mountains and your job. When I was outside today I felt a little of it, the sense of peace, the solitude, as if you're the only one in the world. And the permanence. No matter what man does, the mountains will always be here."

"Unless there's another ice age."

"If there is, I think you've got enough food in your freezer to live through it," she noted.

"Would you be interested in living through it with me?" He couldn't help it, he had to ask. If she said no he could pretend it was just a joke. If she said yes . . .

"Sure."

It wasn't so much what she said, it was how she said it, a little breathlessly, as if her answer surprised her as much as his question did.

"We might be here for a thousand years," he warned.

"I know."

There was a long silence. He pressed his knuckles together. How could he turn her down? An offer to spend eternity with him. Because he had to, because she didn't know what living with him was like, because she couldn't live here and wouldn't want to. "It's different in the summer," he said. "Throngs of people come up to see the view when the snow melts. They can walk up then. There's a hiker's hut halfway up." He sounded like a travel guide, but he couldn't help it. He couldn't stop himself. Maybe it was the bourbon, maybe it was panic. "So there isn't the same sense of solitude. Not like it was before 1645. That's when the first white man arrived with his Indian guide. He was looking for precious gems, but he didn't find any. After him came the pioneers. By the nineteenth century there was even a railroad to bring people up.''

''You know a lot about it.''

''That's it, the history of this mountain in a nutshell. To-night you get the bed all to yourself,'' he said. ''Not that I didn't enjoy sleeping with you...'' He was rambling again. But if he didn't ramble he might get serious. ''My sleeping bag is in the closet behind the bed and I'm going to use it.''

''Didn't we have this conversation before, the last time I was here?'' she asked.

''Maybe. What happened?'' he shifted restlessly on the daybed.

''I fell asleep right here in this chair. I was very comfortable. I don't think I moved all night.''

He smiled in the darkness, remembering how she'd looked with her golden hair framing her face. He knew she hadn't moved because he'd sat there watching her, wondering how this woman had landed in the middle of his solitude. Even now he wondered, what had he done to deserve her?

''You'll be even more comfortable in the bed,'' he assured her.

''Max, you're sick. I'm here to take care of you, because I owe it to you. After my party, I made you sleep on that terrible couch. I'll take the sleeping bag. Later. I'm going to wash the dishes now.''

He was too tired to argue anymore. He tried to roll out of bed and find the sleeping bag, but he got tangled in the blankets. The sound of the water running into the dishpan lulled him into a troubled sleep.

Miranda washed the dishes slowly, dried them carefully and put them back in the cupboard above the sink. When she finished she tiptoed across the room and found the sleeping bag in the closet where he'd said it would be. Then, in the bathroom, she changed into the long underwear her sister had packed for her. It was warm and snug. An extra pillow was stashed on the top shelf of the closet and she made herself comfortable on the carpeted floor near the bed where Max was sleeping soundly.

She was warm, she was comfortable and she was tired. But she couldn't sleep. She was confused, confused by the mixed signals Max was sending her and confused by the mixed reactions she was feeling. She thought she'd made it clear how she felt about him, both subtly and directly. But what good did it do if he didn't feel the same? He wanted her, but he wanted his way of life even more. And who could blame him? It was a good life, a life that challenged him and rewarded him. Who was she to think she could compete with that? She couldn't. And the sooner she got it through her head the better.

The trouble was she liked him, liked hearing him talk, liked seeing the smile light up his face, liked cooking for him. Liked it so much she was willing to make a fool of herself over him. Barging in on his solitude on a flimsy excuse. Yes, it was an excuse. She admitted it. He knew it. He'd been sick before and he'd gotten over it. Without her. And he'd do it again, no matter how much he appreciated her being there, he didn't need her.

Where was her pride? How could she go on this way? The truth was she couldn't. She was leaving tomorrow and nothing, not sleet, not hail or lost boots or childhood disease could bring her back, and she was sure Max felt the same about her and her farm. So why not go to sleep, get through the day tomorrow somehow and then be off? She turned over to block the moonlight that shone on her face.

Somewhere outside in the night the deep muffled hooting of an owl broke the silence. Only it was too early in the season for owls. She slid out of the sleeping bag and padded silently to the side window between the desk and the metal supply cabinets. A shaft of silver moonlight illuminated the snow-covered trees and bushes. The sound came again. *Whoo, whoo, whoo-whoo! Whoo, whoo!* The six-noted hoot of the great horned owl. She raised up on tiptoe and pressed her face against the window. Where was he?

Max stirred in his sleep and awoke to the deep, soft, resonant sound of a faraway owl. He sat up in bed and looked around. No owl and no Miranda. The sleeping bag on the floor was empty. He got out of bed and sat on the coffee table. Then he saw her outlined against the window in moonlight, every curve, every line of her body delineated. His heart pounded, his mouth went as dry as cotton. She was wearing nothing at all. He couldn't move, couldn't speak. He sat and stared and felt the desire well up in him so strong he couldn't fight it off much longer. He gripped the sides of the table. He had to fight it off. She sensed his presence and turned. His eyes lingered on her profile, the upward tilt of her breasts, her flat stomach, the curve of her thighs and her long legs.

The pale moonlight turned her hair to silver and it was then he realized she must be wearing something, and it was her long underwear. The same underwear she was wearing in the catalog. The same catalog that had driven him to distraction ever since he'd seen her picture such a long time ago.

"What's going on?" he asked in a voice like gravel.

"I thought I heard a great horned owl. But isn't it too early?"

"Much too early. Come back to bed." He meant it. He wanted her in bed with him. He wanted to feel the soft knit cotton that covered her body like a second skin, to press her close to him.

But she turned back to the window, still searching for the owl. "There he is," she said at last, "in the fir tree. I wonder what he's looking for."

"It sounds like a mating call to me," he muttered. He ought to know. If he were an owl he'd be out there calling, too. It was a sure sign of spring, the male of the species looking for the female. Max had found the female he was looking for; she was right here in this room. But it wasn't so simple for humans. They didn't mate for life the way owls did and they thought too much.

He rolled back onto his bed and watched her return to his sleeping bag, the moonlight following her like a spotlight. Even then he wasn't sure if she was really wearing the long underwear or nothing at all.

He felt better in the morning. Physically. The rash was subsiding and his temperature was normal. But mentally he was sinking fast. Especially after he called Fred and made arrangements for him to come up and get Miranda in the afternoon.

They went out on the deck together and he showed her how to adjust the vernier to read the barometer. A wind had come up, nothing like the 234 mph record-setting wind, but strong enough that he had to put his hands on her shoulders to steady her as she bent over to look into the telescope.

There wasn't much of a view today. The sky was gray and there was a light mist in the air. She turned to face him and he kept his hands on her shoulders. The humidity made her hair curl in damp tendrils around her face. Lord, if he could only think of a way to keep her here a little longer. He thought of having a relapse, of telling Fred not to come, of quitting his job. But nothing seemed practical, nothing would work. He had to let her go, once and for all. But not without taking a kiss, one last kiss.

He gripped her shoulders tightly and lifted her up on her toes. Her eyes widened. "This is just to say goodbye," he explained, his voice husky with wanting her. "That's all."

"I'm not leaving yet," she said breathlessly, but she met him halfway. More than halfway. He didn't have to take the kiss; she gave it to him freely, fiercely, with her fingers curling through his hair, clinging to him as if she didn't want to leave any more than he wanted her to.

A shaft of desire shot through him that caused him to shake like the balsam fir trees in the wind. She pulled back.

"What's wrong? Are you having a relapse?" Her eyes were like brown velvet, soft with concern.

He shook his head and backed into the door, taking her with him. "I'm having separation anxiety. I don't want to let you go."

"Max," she said before she lost her nerve. "Have you ever thought of getting married again?"

"Not until now." He gave her a long, searching look that seemed to penetrate her very soul. Then his eyes shuttered closed like a camera and she could only think that what he saw there didn't quite measure up.

The roar of the Sno-Cat outside made them look at each other, then away.

"He's early," Max muttered. "What's wrong with that guy? Can't he get the time straight?" He cupped her face with his hands and looked into her eyes. "What's going to happen to you?"

"I'll be fine," she assured him, blinking back the tears that threatened. "And so will you. I realize that now. I see what your life is really like. And I understand how you feel about it. Why you'd never leave." She reached up and touched his cheek, just barely managing a smile. Then she took her bag, half empty now, and her hat from the coat-rack and skittered toward the door.

Before she could open it, Fred did so from the outside and came into the room with a blast of cold, damp air. "How're you doing?" he asked Max. "You don't look so good. Didn't the lady do her stuff?"

"She did her best, but she didn't have enough time. We were just getting started. You came too early."

Fred took off his wool cap. "Sorry about that. But I got to get back. It's different when you have a baby. I baby-sit.

I change diapers." He gave Max a lopsided grin. "And I make formula. You don't know what it's like having a baby around."

No, and I never will, Max thought. How could I have a dozen? I can't even have one and have my job, too.

Fred pulled his hat over his ears. "Ready?" he asked.

Miranda nodded and followed Fred down the wet, slick metal steps, holding onto the railing with her gloved hand. Max shouted at her to be careful, but she didn't hear him. He watched her get into the Sno-Cat next to Fred without a backward glance and he wished *he* could leave it at that, no backward glances and no regrets. But he couldn't.

Chapter Nine

Miranda met Ariel for lunch the next day at the diner on Main Street. It was Ariel's first day back at work. Both boys were finally back at school, but Ariel looked as if she'd been dragged through a ringer, with dark circles under her eyes and cheeks as pale as the white flannel sheets on special in the retail outlet.

"I hope Max wasn't as hard to take care of as Brian and Scott were," Ariel said, running her hand through the limp strands of her brown hair.

"Not really." Miranda studied the menu without seeing the words. The thought that she'd never see Max again had hit her hard this morning. Yesterday she'd been too numb to feel much of anything, but today the reality of it all cut deep and sharp. It was hard to give her order, knowing nothing would fit around the lump in her throat, and the waitress stood shifting from one foot to the other until Miranda gave up and ordered the special—meat-loaf sandwich with a cup of pea soup.

Ariel was looking at her, waiting patiently.

"What?" Miranda asked.

"I asked you how Max was when you left and I told you I've never been so glad to get back to work. You haven't heard anything I've said, have you?"

"Of course I have. I was just thinking."

"About Max or me? Don't bother, I know the answer. You're in love with him, aren't you?"

Miranda felt the color rise to her face. Was it that obvious? "How can you say that? Of course I'm not in love with him. Only a masochist would fall in love with a man who's already in love."

"Max is in love?"

"With his job."

"Oh, no, I don't believe it. Are you sure?"

"I was just up there. I spent a weekend at the weather station. You've seen it. You know how beautiful it is. Well, it's also challenging and changeable and rewarding... and he'll never leave. Not for his first wife, and not for me or anyone else. So if that's what you've been thinking all this time, you can stop." Miranda unfolded her napkin in her lap. "I know you mean well, but this is it, I can't take any more. I like him a lot and he likes me. But I'm not going to see him again. Got it?"

Ariel agreed readily, too readily. Miranda doubted that she'd gotten it or that she'd ever get it. She was determined to get Miranda married off and until she did, she wouldn't rest. If Max didn't work out she'd find another taxidermist or a pharmacist or whatever. But she'd never give up. Miranda could tell by the look in her bleary eyes.

The food came and Ariel continued to look at Miranda as if she were trying to decide what to do next.

"Eat your soup," Miranda advised. "Talk about looking peaked, you've got to take care of yourself or you'll be the next one sick. Can't you get away from the kids, just you and Rob and go somewhere?"

Ariel picked up her spoon and held it in midair. "I don't see how we could. I owe everyone in my baby-sitting coop."

Miranda shrugged. "I'll take them, if it's just for a weekend or something." At the moment she'd do anything to fill the empty hours that lay ahead of her on the weekends.

"That's sweet of you, but they've got soccer games on the weekend, and I work the snack bar."

"I can work the snack bar. How hard can it be?"

Ariel's eyes filled with grateful tears. "You mean it...you'd really do that for me?"

"What are sisters for? Especially after all you've done for me."

Ariel looked down at her lap. "You mean you're not mad at me for inviting Max to your party and inflicting him with chicken pox and fixing you up with the taxidermist?"

"Of course not. You were just doing what you thought was best. But don't do it again, okay? From now on I'm on my own with men. I admit I fell for Max, and maybe I am just a little bit in love with him, but I'm getting over it. It's going to take a while, that's all. And in the meantime I'll baby-sit for you. I'll rototill my fields and I'll get my life back on track. And whenever you feel the urge to play matchmaker, just stifle it, because I'm not in the mood."

Ariel nodded emphatically. "I understand perfectly. You won't catch me even mentioning his name. But can I just ask you how he is?"

Miranda took a sip of water. "He's getting better. His fever is gone and he's not itching so much." In her mind she saw his face covered with spots, his hair matted to his forehead, and she felt her chest tighten as if it were too small for her heart.

"And how did the anti-itch cream work?"

"Fine." The memory of her hand rubbing ointment up and down his back caused her heart to beat in double-time. "And now I've got to get back to work. I'm going to spend more time on my job now. I don't want to sell the farm, but if I have to, I want to have another career to pursue. Maybe I can work my way up to speciality shopper," she said, forcing a smile.

"Good idea," Ariel said thoughtfully. "And I'll talk to Rob about the weekend. If you're sure you want to go through with it, I mean."

Miranda assured her that she did and went back to work. Every time the phone rang with a complaint she thought it might be Max just calling to say thanks. But it never was and he didn't. He understood that she didn't want to see him again or hear from him. She hadn't spelled it out, but he'd understood anyway. If only she could be that strong.

Just talking about him over lunch had brought back the chills up her spine. Otherwise her life was back to grim reality. The skies were an endless gray, the farm was falling apart before her eyes and her job was dull and repetitious. She couldn't help it. She resented every customer who wasn't Max. And that added up to a lot of customers. Mr. Northwood upped his offer to buy the farm, but she told him no and rented a rototiller to plow the back forty. Only the motor stalled and got stuck in the mud. Maybe it was too early to plow, but she had to do something, so she got out the clippers and set upon the apple trees to prune them. She tumbled out of the first tree from the lowest limb, which hurt her dignity more than anything else.

Gratefully she packed her weekend bag to head for Ariel's house in town. Maybe there she'd get a clue about what she was supposed to do with the rest of her life. She sure wasn't getting one where she was.

The kids were waiting with their noses pressed against the front window when she got there. Ariel's face was bright with anticipation and her brother-in-law's grip was warm and friendly when he said goodbye. It was nice to feel wanted, she thought as she cooked spaghetti and meatballs for the boys in her sister's cheerful yellow-and-white kitchen. It was good to be away from the farmhouse, which echoed with memories of Max's presence—from the couch in front of the fireplace where they had sat in the evenings to the big black old-fashioned stove where he'd cooked her pancakes in the morning. Even feeding the horses reminded her of riding through the mud with Max. Everywhere she looked were memories she couldn't escape.

Ariel's house held no memories, and she watched with pleasure as the boys wolfed down their dinner so they could watch the video her sister had rented for them. They went to the family room to watch the movie while Miranda washed the dishes, carefully drying the plates her sister and brother-in-law had received as a wedding present. How easy it was for some people. Ariel and Rob met in high school, got married and had children and lived happily ever after. Others like herself went off to find their fortune and came back empty-handed, but with high hopes. Now those hopes were battered and scarred like her old overnight bag.

And here she was on the crossroads, poised between success and failure, between love and loneliness. It wasn't that she was afraid to take a chance, to accept a challenge. But how long could she keep it up, alone, on her own, accepting challenges and failing to meet them? What was wrong with her anyway?

The front doorbell rang and Miranda dried her hands and went to answer it. She was expecting Ariel's friend with the cash box for tomorrow's snack bar. On her way to the door she ran her hand through her hair and tugged at her oversize natural cotton rag sweater that covered her hips. She pulled the door open but, instead of the friend, it was Max who stood on the doorstep, looking almost as surprised to see her as she was to see him.

"Oh, no," she said.

"Oh, *yes,*" he countered. "I didn't know you'd be here, but I should have guessed. I came to go hunting with Rob."

"Rob? He's not here. He's gone to Stowe with Ariel for the weekend."

"Why didn't he tell me?"

Miranda felt her knees weaken beneath her. Max set his duffel bag down and put his hands under her arms, his fingers grazing the fullness of her breasts. For a moment she looked so distraught he thought she might faint. He lifted her back across the threshold and helped her into the overstuffed flowered chintz easy chair. She pressed her palm against her forehead and closed her eyes.

"I don't believe she did this," she muttered.

Max leaned against the bookshelf that flanked the fireplace. "Miranda," he said, "don't worry about it. I'll leave immediately and we'll pretend it never happened. I'm sorry, I should have known. I should have checked with you to make sure it was on the level. I thought... well, maybe I didn't think or I wouldn't have come. But Rob said... Rob called and told me about this place where he hunts wild turkeys. I never suspected." He frowned at the recollection of the call. Rob had been so friendly, so sincere. And Max was desperate for a diversion, anything to get his mind off Miranda. A weekend in the woods, camping out with a group of men. It had sounded good.

"He said it was just what I needed, some male bonding." He raked his hand through his hair. "Don't worry. I'll leave right away."

She leaned forward in the big chair. "You can't just drive right back. Have you had dinner?"

"No, but..."

"We have lots of spaghetti and meatballs left over." The color was coming back to her cheeks and he thought she'd never looked so beautiful, but, then, he thought that every time he saw her.

"Sounds good." He gave her a slow smile and she smiled back, tentatively at first, then she couldn't help herself, a small hysterical giggle escaped her lips. She held out her arms, her palms up. "What am I going to do with her?" she asked. "I explained the situation to her when I got back from the weather station last week. I told her that you and I had agreed it was all over."

He nodded, but he really wanted to shake his head. Why had they agreed? Why couldn't they see each other? He'd forgotten, forgotten everything but the desire to be with her, here or there or anywhere.

"I didn't expect her to give up, not really," Miranda continued. "I know her too well for that. But I never expected her to do something so blatant, so...so..."

He grinned. "Obvious?"

"Yes. What does she think, that we'll fall into each other's arms the minute we see each other?"

He studied her face and watched the reflection from the table lamp light up her eyes. "That's not a bad idea," he mused.

She stood and walked past him on her way to the kitchen. The look on her face was one of determination. "It's not a good idea, either, but as long as you're here we might as well make the best of it. I'll heat up some spaghetti for you. But I warn you, it's not the kind of food you're used to."

"If you made it, I'll like it," he promised.

He was just spinning the noodles around his fork with expertise when the boys finished watching the video and let out whoops of surprise when they saw him.

"Hey, Max," Scott said dragging a chair next to him at the kitchen table. "Want to come to my soccer game tomorrow?"

Max exchanged a quick glance with Miranda. "Who're you playing?"

"The number one team in the league, but I think we're gonna win. Please, Max, my dad isn't here to watch me. You said you played soccer in high school. And you said sometime you'd show us how to bounce the ball off our heads."

He met Miranda's gaze again and saw her bite her lower lip. "Boys," she said, "leave Max alone. He has other things to do besides go to your game."

"Actually Max has nothing to do at all," he contradicted her. "What about you?"

She leaned back against the refrigerator. "Me? I have to go. I volunteered to take a shift in the snack bar. I'm taking care of the kids so Ariel can get a rest after two weeks at home with the boys."

Before Max could pursue the subject, Brian invited Max to sleep over on the bottom bunk in his room.

Scott jumped out of his chair. "It was my idea. I get to have him in my room."

Hearing that, Brian turned brick-red and threw himself at Scott and they fell on the tiled floor and started to pound each other.

"Boys, boys," Miranda shouted over the din.

Max picked Brian up by his collar and set him on his chair. Then he took Scott and put him, still squirming, on the opposite side of the table.

"Believe it or not no one's ever fought over me before," he told Miranda, who was watching the whole scene still glued to the refrigerator door.

"You'd better take advantage of it while you can," she said.

"You mean I've got to choose one of them. Is that all right with you?"

"I can handle it if you can," she said lightly.

Max shrugged, but in his heart there was hope, hope sprouting like a seed under the New England snow. It was ridiculous and it didn't make sense, but here she was and where she was there was hope. One more chance to see her, to pretend that anything was possible between them. The last chance, maybe, but still a chance. To make it fair, he tossed a coin, which decided that he'd sleep in Brian's room.

Scott got up out of his chair, his lower lip trembling. "Then I get him tomorrow night."

Miranda exchanged a long, helpless look with Max. She ought to say no, Max is going home tomorrow after the game, but she didn't have the heart to do it. He'd have to tell them himself. But he didn't. He asked them about their team, who sponsored it and what positions they played. Miranda picked up the dish towel and dried a glass until it shone.

She couldn't say she wasn't happy to have him here. Maybe happy wasn't the right word. It was more a feeling of being alive again after a week of feeling as if she'd been frozen in the snow. The look in his eyes made every nerve tingle, the same nerve ends she'd thought were dead and buried. She knew and he knew that he was not staying just to see a soccer game. They both knew that electricity still crackled between them, right here in the kitchen.

When Miranda announced it was bedtime, Brian insisted Max come with him and get into the lower bunk so he could hang his head over and look into Max's face. Miranda stood in the doorway looking at them, the little boy on top and the big man, his knees drawn up to his chest to fit into the bed. She climbed up the ladder to plant a kiss on Brian's cheek, even though he ducked under the covers and pretended to rub it off immediately afterward.

She knew Max was looking at her as she came down the ladder. He'd pulled the sheet up to his chin and his blue eyes had a wicked gleam. "Well?" he said.

"Go ahead," Brian urged. "You kissed me, you gotta kiss Max, too."

She leaned over and gave Max a light kiss on his cheek, but the faint scent of pine soap and the smell of the mountain air that clung to his skin were her undoing. She hesitated just a moment and he took her in his arms and kissed her with a tenderness that touched her deeply. She heard Brian's muffled laughter and then she heard Scott calling for a drink of water from his bedroom but she couldn't move. She was caught, trapped again, wanting to sink down into bed with him, to taste his lips again, to see where it would lead.

If it hadn't been for the boys she would have done it. But if it hadn't been for the boys, he wouldn't be there at all. So she staggered out of the room to get Scott his water, then went to the master bedroom, where she fell forward into her sister's king-size bed.

She was so tired she couldn't move. Tired of struggling to make ends meet, tired of fighting off the attraction between her and Max. Every time she saw him he was sweeter, kinder and more diabolically attractive. If this really were the last time she was going to see him (how many times had she thought *that?*) then just this once she was going to stop fighting and give in and enjoy having him around.

There was a certain family feeling to the whole situation. She and Max as surrogate parents. Only most husbands didn't sleep on the bottom bunk in the children's room; they slept in the master bedroom, next to the wife. She stretched her arm out across the bed. No, no one there.

Max certainly had a knack for dealing with kids. He said he wanted a dozen children, and she had no doubt he could handle them. If he were around. If he weren't working on top of a mountain and unavailable for such family crises as chicken pox. The tension eased from her body as she convinced herself to let herself go, play family this weekend and suffer the consequences later.

Saturday morning found Max in the kitchen wearing corduroy pants and a plaid wool hunting shirt, flipping his famous pancakes in the air to the delight of the boys. The smell of maple syrup bubbling on the stove filled the air with its familiar sweetness. Miranda sat at the table and let him do all the work, laughing with the boys as he flipped a pancake on Scott's head. No wonder Ariel was so anxious for

Miranda to exchange her solitary life for marriage and a family. The warmth, the closeness, had an undeniable appeal and as she looked around the table she felt longing well inside her.

When the boys had stuffed themselves and gone upstairs to change into their shorts, shin guards and cleats, Max sat across the table from Miranda. The look in his eyes told her he felt it, too, so badly it hurt.

She tore her eyes from his and stirred her coffee. "Have you ever been hunting before?" she asked,

"Never," he said. "But the thought of camping out and sleeping in a sleeping bag under the stars appealed to me."

Miranda nodded. "You might even have bagged a wild turkey. Rob always comes home with something."

"So it wasn't a total fabrication. There are wild turkeys and your brother-in-law does go hunting."

"Yes. And he probably meant it when he asked you to go along. But then I offered to baby-sit and I guess he forgot to call and cancel the hunting party." She sipped her coffee and gazed at him over the edge of her cup. "Or at least that's the story they'll use when they come back on Sunday night and find you here." She shook her head. "I can't believe Rob would do anything like this on purpose. Now Ariel, she's a different story. She'd stoop to lying, cheating and playing on my sympathy if she thought it would serve her purpose. Now that I think of it, she probably engineered the whole thing. I can't wait to get my hands on her."

Max got up and rinsed his cup in the sink. "I'm sorry I barged in on you like this, but I'm having a better time than shooting wild turkeys. The kids are great, the beds are too short, but there are other fringe benefits." He gave her a sideways look that curled her toes inside her soft white pure wool socks and sucked the breath out of her.

Abruptly she got to her feet and had already started for the living room when she felt his hand on her hip. He gave her a firm pat on the bottom, the kind of gesture that telegraphed familiarity, intimacy and, when his hand lingered, it signaled desire, too. Casually, he followed her to the living room, where she tripped over the soccer ball in the middle of the floor, then lunged for her hooded storm coat, which she'd left on the arm of the chair.

Outside the temperature was rising and icicles were melting. There was a hint of spring in the air. So *that* was what was wrong with her, this light-headedness and giddiness, it was spring fever. It couldn't be anything else. Hadn't she promised herself she'd keep her emotions under wraps?

Once at the field they split up, the boys to the field, Miranda to the snack bar. Max disappeared. A ton of hot dogs simmered in a stainless-steel vat, waiting to be put into buns and stored in a warming tray. By craning her neck she could see a corner of the playing field, but she never saw the boys or Max until she was relieved an hour later.

She wandered out to the field where Brian and Scott were running up and down, stumbling, falling, but never stopping. And Max was pacing up and down the field, shouting words of encouragement. Miranda found a seat on a wooden bench, stretched her legs out in front of her and inhaled the fragrance of the damp earth. On a day like this, ripe with the promise of spring, she could believe all things were possible, a farm that paid its way, a husband to help her run it and children who ran and fell and picked themselves up again. Could anyone want more?

Max did, she thought, walking out onto the field, clapping enthusiastically even though she had no idea who had won. Max wanted a job that provided him with a built-in life-style. One that challenged him on a level that ordinary life didn't. And she couldn't compete with that. Nobody could.

On the way home they stopped at a restaurant that specialized in Southern-fried chicken. The boys never stopped talking about the game, reliving every minute with Max chiming in.

"Guess where we're sleeping tonight," Scott blurted, his eyes shining with excitement.

"If it's okay with Aunt Miranda," Max cautioned.

"If it's okay with you, we're going to sleep outside in Max's tent in our sleeping bags."

"Isn't it kind of cold?" Miranda asked.

"We've got sleeping bags," Brian informed her. "We won't be cold."

"Since I was planning to sleep out this weekend I brought my down bag and my three-man tent. I thought we'd set it up in the backyard. Of course you're welcome to join us," he added with a smile.

Miranda declined politely, picturing four people in a three-man tent and realizing just how cozy it would be. Later, from the window at the kitchen above the sink, she watched them pound the stakes into the earth to hold the tent in place. The temperature was falling even as their spirits rose. The boys came racing in to get their sleeping bags from their closets. It was only seven o'clock, but they told her they had to go to bed.

An hour after that Miranda went outside in her parka with a flashlight in her hand. She unzipped the flap and looked inside. Max was in the middle, his arms folded under his head, his blond-brown hair standing on end. The boys flanked him on either side, blinking up owlishly at her.

"We're telling ghost stories," Scott informed her.

"I hope you won't have nightmares," she said.

Max raised up on one elbow and grinned at her. "If we do we'll come and get into bed with you."

She raised her eyebrows in alarm. "All three of you?"

"Only those who are really scared."

Instead of answering she zipped the flaps shut.

"Aunt Miranda," Brian called. She unzipped the flaps again. "There's room for you in here." He squeezed to one side, leaving a six-inch gap between Max and himself.

Miranda smiled at him. "Thanks, but I think it's too cold out here for me."

Max patted the space firmly with the palm of his hand. "I think I can keep you warm," he said, his mouth curving up into an inviting smile.

Miranda pictured herself squeezed between them, her body pressed against Max, his arm around her, the heat from his body infusing hers with heated desire. For a moment she hesitated, torn between the hard ground, his hard body and good sense. Then she shook her head firmly and went back to the house. She prowled around aimlessly, closing the curtains, turning down the heat, fighting the urge to go out and check on them again. Knowing she wanted to see Max again, knowing she was hooked on his smile and his low-key sense of humor.

Finally she took a shower in the master bedroom, got into her sister's bed, propped herself on a mound of ruffled pillows and turned on the late-night local news. Three teenagers were accused of stealing from the town dump. A Lake Waukasha councilman resigned in an income tax scandal. And there was a late bulletin from the Mount Henry State Park. Two hikers were lost in a sudden snowstorm in the area below the weather station. The forest service had been called in, but snow and sleet were hampering the rescue efforts.

Miranda jumped out of bed and threw on her sister's quilted robe. Snow on Mount Henry when it was almost spring here? She ran to the backyard and opened the flaps again.

"Max," she whispered.

He sat up straight, instantly awake. "What's up?"

"I just heard on the news. Some hikers are lost on Mount Henry."

He got out of his sleeping bag and jackknifed onto his knees. Crawling out of the tent, he straightened and put his hands on her shoulders. He looked into her eyes, a deep frown on his face. "What happened?"

"There was a sudden snowstorm. They've called in the park rangers, but the visibility is terrible."

"I'll bet they're not dressed for the weather. That's the way it happens, especially in the spring. I'll have to get back there and help. I know the mountain better than the rangers."

Miranda shivered, thinking of the hikers lost on the mountain, knowing how fast the weather could change. She walked into the house with him and helped him carry his bag and his boots to the car. She wished he didn't have to go, now, in the middle of the night, but she knew he would, whether it was expected of him or not. Just as he'd helped her bottle syrup. It wasn't his job, but he did it anyway. That's the way he was and that was the thing she loved about him. Not the only thing, she realized. Just one of many things.

He rolled down his window and she leaned over to say goodbye. "Tell the boys I'm sorry," he said. "You'd better wake them and bring them in."

She nodded. "Is there any danger you'd get lost, too, I mean, if it's that bad?"

He took her fingers in his and rubbed them between his palms to warm them. "Not a chance," he assured her. "I know where to look. I've been up and down those trails a dozen times. We've never lost a hiker yet, or a weatherman." He brought her fingers to his lips and kissed them. "I'll be in touch."

She stood in the driveway watching his taillights disappear down the slick streets and then there was silence. Her teeth chattering, she hugged her arms to her body and hurried to the backyard, unzipped the flaps and looked down at the boys, their eyes closed tightly in sleep. They were breathing evenly, unaware that their leader—their hero—had gone off to be a real hero.

Miranda ducked down and entered the tent, crawling into Max's sleeping bag between the boys, just where he'd left it. She zipped the flaps shut. The warmth of his body still clung to the lining of the sleeping bag. She breathed deeply. The smell of his clothes and the all-male scent of his body lingered. She snuggled deeper into the sleeping bag, wishing he were there with her.

The only sound was the deep steady breathing of her nephews. The dim light from the sky glowed through the blue nylon of the tent, casting a pale glow on their faces. Where was Max? On the turnpike? Halfway across the state by now? She knew what he must be thinking about. His thoughts were with the lost hikers, tracing their steps down the mountain in his mind.

If she were lost there was no one she'd rather have out looking for her than Max. She lay awake for a long time, remembering the touch of his lips against her fingers and the sound of his voice. It was time to face the fact that she loved him, she told herself as night turned into morning. Because if she didn't, she couldn't get over him. And she had to get over him because he didn't love her. Not enough, anyway.

Chapter Ten

Max drove as fast as he dared, down silent roads in the dark night. It was cold but there was no snow, not until he got to the highway that led to the town of Mount Henry. Then it covered the pavement with a blanket of white and drifted on the shoulders of the road. He knew what had happened. He listened to a report on his car radio and pieced the rest of it together with his knowledge of the weather and the terrain.

It must have been a sunny spring morning. Two hikers in shorts and shirtsleeves parked at the foot of the mountain with plans to hike to the top, then suddenly, halfway up, the temperature dropped. The barometer fell and out of nowhere snow flurries appeared. The hikers had probably started down and the flurries had turned into a full-fledged storm. Six inches of snow in an hour, covering the trails, blotting out the landmarks.

They must have lost the trail. Wearing ordinary hiking shoes, they'd slip and slide. Then it turned dark and although the snow had stopped, they wouldn't be able to see their hands in front of them. Yes, he knew the scenario. At the station at the foot of the mountain, Max stopped to talk to the rangers and to a radio reporter who added some details to the story. They'd covered the south slope and were trying to decide what to do next. Max said he'd drive up the road as far as he could, park and take off into the woods to the east. He had a flashlight and his all-weather boots.

He didn't get any farther than a half mile up the mountain before he felt his tires slipping. He stopped right there in the road and left the car. He tightened the bindings on his boots and thanked God and Miranda Morrison for the reinforced rubber soles. If it hadn't been for Miranda he wouldn't have these high-top, waterproof boots. If it weren't for Miranda he wouldn't know about long underwear or real maple syrup or chicken and dumplings on a raw winter night. And that wasn't all he'd learned from her.

He'd learned to love again. Yes, he loved her, loved her so much he wanted the best for her, and that wasn't him. Outside in the elements he felt nothing, only the cold wind in his face and the snow underfoot as he tramped across the slope of the mountain, making switchbacks in the snow on his way to the trail. He welcomed the cold and the wind and the challenge of the mountain. Without them he might start feeling again, feeling the loss and the pain.

He knew exactly where the trail was, even without using the beam from his flashlight, but somehow he was wrong— the trail wasn't where it was supposed to be. Another half hour of wasted time while the hikers could be suffering from hypothermia, unprepared for a night of freezing temperatures. He had to find them soon before frostbite set in.

When he finally stumbled across the snowy trail it was easier going than walking overland, because when he found the trail he also found their footprints. He yelled, he called their names, but the darkness swallowed up his voice. He was running down the trail, slipping, sliding and yelling again, until he finally heard an answer, faint, so faint he wasn't sure it was real. Then he saw them, huddled under a low fir, a man and a woman. He pulled them up from the ground and peeled off his jacket and then his sweater to give to them. Back along the trail they followed close behind him, hands linked together. Then they plowed their way over tangled branches and snow-covered bushes to his car.

They laughed and cried, almost hysterical with relief. They'd thought no one would ever find them and they'd freeze to death before morning. He backed down to the turnaround and drove to the ranger station. There the rescue squad radioed to the other searchers and gave the couple emergency first aid.

Max declined the coffee they offered him. The reporter from the radio station interviewed him and he was able to slip in some background information on the mountain and its unique weather patterns while he played down his own part in the rescue. He took his jacket and sweater and went out to his car.

Daylight was breaking over the mountain, turning the new snow to pale pink and orange. He sat in his car for a long time, not feeling the cold that crept in and permeated the leather seat cushions. He wished he could drive back to Vermont and get back into that sleeping bag and take up where he left off. But if he went back now to the warmth of a sleeping bag and the one woman who could make his life complete, he'd be perpetuating a dream. A dream that he and Miranda could have a life, somehow, somewhere. And that just wasn't true. She knew it and so did he.

Some people thought he had a half-time job, but it was a full-time commitment. One that he took seriously. Wives wanted their husbands to be committed to them and he didn't blame them. That was what Miranda deserved. Someone who'd be there when she needed him, to feed the horses, collect the sap or take care of her when she was sick.

As Fred said, "It's different now." Babies, diapers and kids growing up. He'd want to be there. He couldn't stand not to. He also couldn't stand to think of someone else playing that role in her life. He drove to his apartment a few miles away and called Ariel's house, but no one answered. He was almost relieved. He didn't want to say goodbye. Not again.

He fell asleep with his clothes on, dreaming of kids being lost in the snow, his kids. When he woke up it was mid-morning and he called again. This time Ariel answered, full of questions and concern. They'd seen the report on TV last night at their hotel and had heard him on the car radio that morning. They were so proud of him and so relieved that everyone was okay.

He asked to speak to Miranda. "She's not here, she went home. She said she had a lot to catch up on." There was a long pause. "She said to say thanks for everything. Whatever happened this weekend, I don't know, but the boys had a great time. I'm sorry you got stuck with them."

"We had a lot of fun. They're great kids."

"Rob wants to apologize for the mix-up about the hunting trip."

"No problem."

"Miranda thinks this was another one of my schemes, but it wasn't, honestly."

"Don't worry about it."

"I'm worried about Miranda. When we got here this morning she was all packed up to leave. She heard you on the radio so she knew you rescued the hikers. Then she took off just like that."

"I'll call her," he said.

"I've been calling her, but she doesn't answer."

"Maybe she's outside."

Ariel agreed and Max made arrangements to come by and pick up his tent and sleeping bag and then he hung up. His every instinct cried out to get into the car and drive to the farm, but he couldn't do that. He had to let her go, now, before it was too late. He would tell her what had happened and say goodbye. She'd understand.

He called all day, but she never answered. Maybe she never got there, maybe she fell into a pothole on that rutted road to the farm. Or maybe the horse stepped on her again and she couldn't get back to the house. Knowing Miranda, she'd crawl through the mud on her hands and knees before she'd ask for help.

He knew how proud she was of being independent, yet they worked well together. In the fields or in the house. And they had fun together, like this past weekend. He'd miss her. He missed her now, so much there was an empty feeling in the pit of his stomach. If only he could hear her voice. If only she'd answer. Finally, at dusk, she did.

"Where've you been?" he demanded. "I've been trying to call you all day."

"Outside. I thought you'd sleep all day. You deserve to after what you went through. I heard you on the radio. You made it sound like nothing."

"It was nothing. I just followed their footsteps. They were right where I thought they'd be."

"That's not what the man on the radio said. He said it was a heroic rescue."

"It's part of my job."

"Even on your day off?"

"Anytime. That's why..."

"You don't have to explain. I know what you're going to say. I'm glad you called. Goodbye, Max." She hung up before he could say any more. Before he could tell her he loved her.

The finality of her farewell sunk in slowly. It was still sinking in when he returned to the weather station. The excitement of the rescue had faded away and he was back to being an observer of the world's worst weather. Only the worst weather had become the best. Spring had come to the mountain, melting the snow and causing wildflowers to push their way up through the cracks in the mica schist.

The sight of the new leaves and the smell of the damp earth caused Max to feel restless. Instead of enjoying the isolation, he felt trapped, what some weathermen called rock fever, caused by an inability to get off the rock.

The local radio station called. The producer had been so happy with Max's report on the rescue, he wanted to do a short special on the weather station and what went on up there. Instead of Max's going down to the studio, however, they did the interview over the telephone, live. He wondered if Miranda heard it. Fred heard it and he called, but Miranda didn't. He'd tried to make it interesting, but maybe she wasn't interested in anything he said anymore.

He could have called her. He could have called her at work and ordered something. He thumbed through the catalog, stopping at the page with her picture, thinking of how it affected him when he saw her wearing her long underwear with the moonlight shining on her. Thinking of how no picture could capture the light that shone from her eyes, or the curve of her lips when she smiled at him. The touch of her skin, the silkiness of her hair brushing his cheek, were not something you could see in a picture.

He should have looked forward to getting off the mountain at the end of the week and going home. But his apartment had never been home to him. If he had a home it was here on the mountain. But not anymore. He paced, he wished for a storm to blot out the magnificent views, because he had no one to share them with. But the weather just wouldn't cooperate. Each day was more beautiful than the last. With his binoculars he could see the ships in the Portland harbor. If only Miranda were here to see them, too.

Miranda was at work during the day, and instead of enjoying the beautiful spring weather, she was hunched over her desk, trying to make sense of lost items, mistakes in billing and back orders on trapper blankets. She wanted to leave her desk in order when she quit her job.

She'd finally decided to sell the farm. Mr. Northwood had made her one last offer and she'd accepted. Now she could quit her job and do whatever she liked. The problem was that what she liked was to work the farm, put in the Christmas trees and increase apple production. But she had come to the reluctant conclusion that she couldn't have it all, and that her freedom was more important than the farm. Now it was up to her to decide what to do with that freedom.

She hadn't told anyone she'd sold the farm. Not even Ariel. Ariel would have a dozen suggestions. She'd tell her to buy a little house in town and then open a coffee shop or an art gallery. Maybe even a bed-and-breakfast. All of which would be assets to the town, but none of which appealed to Miranda. She thought of calling Max to tell him but she didn't. She heard him on the radio, his voice so deep and resonant and so professional-sounding she wondered if it was the same person who'd paced the soccer field yelling words of encouragement to her nephews.

His love of the mountains and his understanding of the weather came through loud and clear on the radio and filled her with awe. It also filled her with longing. Longing to see him, to hear his voice up close and in person and to feel his arms around her, his lips on hers.

She'd asked him if she should sell the farm and she hadn't forgotten his answer. "You have to do what's right for you." She was alone in this decision, as she was in life. And a farm was no place for a woman alone. At least not her. She'd given it her all and it wasn't enough. She'd never believed it could happen, but she'd come to the end of her rope.

It seemed to her that the farm had never looked more beautiful. The apple trees were budding, the daffodils her grandmother had planted years ago were poking their green stalks through the earth along the front driveway. It made her ache inside to know she wouldn't be there next year when they came up. She had to get away. She couldn't stand to walk around the fields one more time. She put the horses out to graze and she called in sick. In a way she was sick. She had spring fever. Then she called Ariel, who hadn't left for work yet.

"I'm going crazy. I've got to get away from here," she confessed.

"What's wrong?" Ariel asked anxiously.

"I don't know. I just know I can't stay here another minute. I'm going to take a walk somewhere."

"How about up to the top of Mount Henry?" Ariel suggested innocently.

There was a brief pause. "Do you think that's a good idea?"

"I think it's a great idea. They say it's beautiful in the spring."

"I've always wanted to see the wildflowers," Miranda said thoughtfully.

"Who are you kidding, Miranda?" Ariel asked gently. "This is your sister, remember? You've always wanted to see the wildflowers and you've always wanted to see Max."

"Max made his choice," Miranda reminded her. "He chose his job and not me, and I don't want to force him to tell me that again. It's too painful."

"I know, I know. But just give him one more chance."

Miranda hung up. She didn't know what she'd say if she saw Max again. She didn't know if she'd tell him she'd sold the farm and that she was free to live anywhere she wanted. Anywhere *he* wanted. She didn't know if she'd tell him she'd rather have him half time than anybody else full-time.

She gripped the steering wheel of her car tightly as she imagined coming face-to-face with Max. Her hands shook and her mind was spinning. When she arrived there were only a few cars in the parking lot. The sun was warm on her shoulders and the sky was clear, only a stray cirrus cloud or two scudding across the sky. Mindful of changing weather conditions, she wore hiking boots, long pants, a turtleneck polo shirt and a windbreaker tied around her waist. Max had told her the easiest climb was on the south face, a two-hour hike to the summit at the most. She strapped a day pack on her back and started out.

But she wasn't accustomed to the thin mountain air and she climbed slowly, pausing frequently to drink from the canteen in her pack. The sun was high in the sky and her fate was in the hands of the gods . . . and Max.

On the top of the mountain Max walked back and forth on the observation deck, without noticing the clouds or the view or the new vegetation beneath him. He was thinking about the visit he'd had two days ago from the producer and the program director of the local radio station. They'd come to make him an offer he couldn't refuse. They wanted him to be their staff meteorologist. He didn't even have to quit his job if he didn't want to. They'd set him up with a fax machine and a computer with a modem. He'd do all his reports from right where he was. Wherever he was.

"Wherever I am?" he'd asked, leaning forward in his chair.

"Anywhere," they'd assured him. "That's the way it's done these days."

He'd looked around the four walls, out the window to the mountains in the distance, and he'd known it was time to say goodbye to this mountain, to this solitude, to the pursuit of observing the weather. From now on he'd report the weather from somewhere else. It was time to take part in life instead of just observing it.

He'd accepted and then he'd quit his job.

And now it was time to tell Miranda. On this beautiful spring morning he called her, but she wasn't at work today. He pictured her at home, outside in the field, when she didn't pick up the phone. Maybe she was playing hooky. He called again. No answer.

* * *

On the trail, Miranda saw wild lupine growing in the crevices where glaciers had once passed. She touched the layers of rock and she pictured the mountain as an ancient seabed. It was so awesome she didn't notice the clouds that gathered until a few raindrops spattered her face.

Fortunately she had her waterproof windbreaker, guaranteed to shed water like a duck's back, and her wool stocking cap in her pocket. This was a good time to test her gear, she thought as she continued upward. She pictured the surprised look on Max's face when she appeared at his door, slightly wet, slightly tired, but on her own, no car, no Sno-Cat. And she'd decided what to say. She was going to make him an offer he couldn't refuse.

If he said no, she wasn't sure what she'd do. Turn around and walk back down the mountain in the rain? If only it weren't raining quite so hard now. Maybe she should have stayed home and made this offer by phone.

Up at six-thousand feet, the rain turned to hail as Max watched the temperature fall. He realized it probably wasn't hailing in Vermont, but why in the hell didn't she come into her house and answer the phone? At dusk he gave up and called Ariel. She told him Miranda had left hours ago to hike up the mountain.

He asked her which way she was coming, what trail she was taking. Ariel didn't know, she had no idea. Her voice was shaky. He didn't mention the hail. "Don't worry," he said. "I'll find her."

"Okay," she said, relieved.

He didn't have a hard hat. He'd never seen one in the catalog. But if he ever needed one it was today. The hail was coming down in chunks the size of golf balls, bouncing off his head and shoulders as he made his way down the mountain. He could only hope it wasn't hailing below or that she'd made it as far as the hiker's hut. Had he told her about the hut? Had he told her the south face was the easiest to climb?

He berated himself as he slid in the pebbles of hail as the trail crisscrossed the slope. Why hadn't he called her sooner? Yesterday? Why did it take a radio station to show him how to have everything he wanted, including Miranda? Didn't he know by now that she came first, ahead of his job, ahead of everything? What if she'd been knocked down by the hailstones? They were certainly big enough.

When he got to the hiker's hut he was staggering, dizzy and disoriented. He wrenched the door open to find her huddled in the corner, wet and cold, her eyes wide with wonder at seeing him there. She jumped up and threw her arms around him and they spun crazily on the dirt floor of the small hut, clinging to each other as if they were the last humans alive.

"How did you find me?" she demanded.

Gently he removed her hands from around the back of his neck while her face blurred before his eyes. "Can we sit down before I *fall* down?"

"What's wrong? Were you hit by a hailstone?"

"About a hundred hailstones. About this size." He made a circle with his thumb and forefinger.

"Oh Max, I'm so sorry. I was out for a hike, that's all. It was such a beautiful day." She sat down next to him on the wooden bench that flanked the rustic wooden table. "I wanted to see those layers of rock you told me about." Now that he was here next to her all the words she'd been going to say vanished from her mind. She'd lost her nerve.

"You mean you weren't coming to see me?" he asked, his brow furrowed.

"Of course not."

Her lips trembled and he wanted to kiss her, to tell her she was going to be his forever. "You were going to climb all the way up this mountain and never even stop by to say hello?"

"Well, maybe just hello. How did you know I was here?"

"Guess."

She clenched her teeth. "I should have known. What did she say?"

"Only that you were out for a hike. I called her to ask where you were. I had something to tell you, something to ask you."

Suddenly she found her courage. She met his gaze. "Me, too. I've got something to tell you, too. I . . . I've sold the farm and I'm going to quit my job. I'm free for the first time in my life to do whatever I want, to live wherever I want. . . ."

He heard the wind rattle the windows of the tiny shack and felt her words knock the breath out of him. "Sold the farm? Why?"

"Because I couldn't handle it alone. I was fooling myself thinking I could."

He buried his head in his hands. Maybe he had a concussion after all.

"What's wrong?"

"Nothing. It's your farm. *Was* your farm."

There was a long silence while the hail drummed on the roof.

"What do you have to tell me?" she asked softly.

He raised his head and looked into her dark troubled gaze. "I quit my job. I'm going to be the weatherman for WKEZ."

Her mouth fell open, her lips formed the shape of a round O but she was too stunned to speak for several moments. "What's that?" she asked.

"That's the radio station in Manchester. I can send in my reports from anywhere by phone. I'll have my instruments and a fax machine and a computer with a modem. That's how it's done these days."

"Where will you send them in from?"

He shrugged. He couldn't tell her he'd thought he'd send them in from the farm, the farm that she'd just sold. Now there were two of them on the loose, free-floating bodies looking for a home.

"Can you get the farm back?" he asked.

She bit her lip. "I don't know. Can you get your job back?"

"I don't want it back. After you left it was never the same. I couldn't stand the solitude. I know I told you I loved it, but I love you more. There, that's what I had to tell you," he said, his head heavy, his heart aching, afraid she didn't feel the same.

"Max," she said, alarmed. "You must have a concussion. From the hailstones. Your eyes are dilated, you're delirious. You said you loved me." She held his head between her hands, forcing him to look at her, hoping he'd say it again.

He shook his head and crushed her to him. "I'm not delirious," he assured her. "I *do* love you. If we can't have the farm we'll buy a house somewhere. *Anywhere* as long as you'll live with me. Marry me, be the mother of my children, all twelve of them," he murmured into her ear.

Tears came to her eyes and flowed down her cheeks. She hoped he knew what he was saying, because it was what she wanted to hear. She gripped his shoulders fiercely and kissed him with all the passion she'd kept bottled up. His lips were warm now, as if he'd never been in a hailstorm.

With a surge of energy he lifted her onto his lap and kissed her slowly, starting with the sensitive spots behind her ears and moving to her eyelids and the tip of her nose.

"Don't ever do that again," he said, his lips against her cheek. "If you love me."

"I love you," she assured him. "What shouldn't I do?"

"Go out in a hailstorm without a hard hat."

She ran her fingers through his thick blond hair. "What about you?"

"I won't, either," he promised solemnly, and he kissed her again to seal the bargain.

When the hail stopped they trudged back up to the observatory. Miranda changed into dry clothes Max loaned her and she called Ariel.

"He found me," Miranda reported when her sister answered the phone.

"And now what?" her sister demanded.

"Now we're going to have a glass of sherry."

"When are you coming home?"

"That's the bad news. I don't have a home. I sold the farm."

"*What?* How could you?"

"I thought it was a good idea at the time. Even you thought it was a good idea. I just couldn't make it on my own, but things have changed...." She smiled as Max came up behind her and circled her waist with his arm. "I'm not on my own anymore. Max and I ..."

"I mean, how could you sell the farm without my signature? I own the rights to the stables, at least that's what Grandpa always said."

"He did?"

"He knew I had no place to keep the horses in town, and he wanted to be sure I'd always have a place to ride. But I don't know if it's legal, there was nothing about it in the will."

"I'll find out," Miranda said. She was afraid to tell Max, for fear he'd get his hopes up, now that she knew he loved the farm as much as she did. But she knew she'd have to try to get the farm back, one way or another.

That night they watched the moon shining on the ice on the distant mountain summits and talked about the past and the future, avoiding any mention of where they'd live. Max felt guilty for letting her sell the farm, she felt guilty for not telling him before she signed the papers. In the morning she left early, after kissing him goodbye. The air was still and clear and she clung to him for just one more kiss, one more assurance that he loved her with or without her farm.

She didn't tell him where she was going. She didn't tell him she was scared she'd fail again, fail to recover the farm they both loved. When she arrived in town she went into the bank and opened her safety deposit box. At the polished table, in the quiet of the vault, she read over the deed to the farm, handwritten in her grandfather's precise old-fashioned penmanship.

Tears filled her eyes as she went over the details, the rights of way, the boundaries and the riparian rights to the brook that ran through the property. Then she saw it, an addendum, something her grandfather, always scrupulously fair and kind, had added to insure that Ariel would not be left out. She'd found what she was looking for. Joy filled her heart as she locked the deed back into the metal box. She wouldn't have to throw herself on Mr. Northwood's mercy. She wouldn't have to offer to buy back the farm at an inflated price.

She drove the few blocks to Green Mountain Merchants and went directly to Mr. Northwood's office on the first floor. He was there, behind his desk, wearing his usual button-down flannel shirt and corduroy pants from the December catalog.

"Well, Miranda," he said, looking up at her through his wire-rimmed glasses. "What can I do for you?"

"You can give me back my farm," she blurted. "I'll write you a check right now for the same amount you gave me last week."

He gave her a thin-lipped smile. "So you found out about the road."

"What road?"

"Oh, come now. I knew it would come out sooner or later. The road that runs along the east side of your farm. The reason they've never filled in the potholes is that there's going to be a four-lane highway there. Isn't that what you've come to tell me?"

Stunned, she rocked back on her heels. "No, it isn't." She swallowed hard. "I've come to tell you I had no right to sell it to you. It's not completely mine. My sister has rights to the east side, where the stables are, to keep her horses there. That's what it says in the deed."

His face turned the color of the manila folder on his desk. "Are you sure about this? Do you mean you sold it to me under false pretenses?"

"I didn't mean to. I didn't know about it until today. It would have come out in the title search. But it's only fair to tell you about it now." She took her checkbook from her purse and scribbled the amount he'd paid her for the farm and his name on a check and handed it to him.

"I suppose this means you'll sell your maple syrup direct from a stand along the highway and bypass us altogether."

"Yes," Miranda said, her hopes soaring, "along with my Christmas trees and apples. But I'll leave the clothing to you. And the complaint department. It's all yours."

She almost skipped down the hall toward her office to say goodbye to her friends and to clean out her desk. She told them they were all invited to the wedding and then she stopped by the retail store before Ariel heard the news secondhand and not from her.

Ariel was kneeling behind a display of scented soap and bath towels. When she looked up at her sister, her face puckered into an anxious frown.

"You know you were right about your horses," Miranda said, unable to keep the tears of happiness from welling up in her eyes. "I've got the farm back thanks to you and Grandpa. And you've got a place to keep your horses forever."

"What about Max? Was I right when I told you to go up there yesterday?"

"Yes," Miranda admitted. "And to show our appreciation we're going to name our first child after you."

Ariel stood slowly, her eyes wide with surprise. Then, in a burst of joy, she let out a whoop that startled the customers and then she hugged her sister tightly.

Still in a daze of happiness, Miranda drove home along the pitted road soon to become four lanes. When she drove up her driveway lined with spring daffodils she saw Max sitting on the front steps waiting for her. She ran into his arms and he hugged her to him. "Is anything wrong?" she asked, her voice muffled against his sweater.

"That's what I came to find out. I figured if things didn't work out, you'd need consolation and if they did, you'd need someone to celebrate with." He held her by the shoulders and looked deep into her eyes. "Which is it?"

Her smile said it all. Triumph, love and happiness. The details could wait till later.

"This may not be appropriate," Max said, sweeping her up in his arms. "But I'm going to carry you over the threshold. Right now."

She threw her arms around him and her dark eyes brimmed over with happiness. "And then what?"

"And then I'm going to kiss you until you're senseless."

"That won't take much. I'm almost senseless now. Then what?"

"Then I'm going to make you a big breakfast."

She nuzzled his chin. "A man after my own heart."

"That's me," he said and he carried her through the door.

* * * * *

What a year for romance!

Silhouette has five fabulous romance collections coming your way in 1993. Written by popular Silhouette authors, each story is a sensuous tale of love and life—as only Silhouette can give you!

Three bachelors are footloose and fancy-free...until now.
(March)

Heartwarming stories that celebrate the joy of motherhood.
(May)

Put some sizzle into your summer reading with three of Silhouette's hottest authors.
(June)

Take a walk on the dark side of love—with tales just perfect for those misty autumn nights.
(October)

Share in the joy of yuletide romance with four award-winning Silhouette authors.
(November)

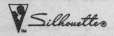

A romance for all seasons—it's always time for romance with Silhouette!

PROM93

Silhouette Books has done it again!

Opening night in October has never been as exciting! Come watch as the curtain rises and romance flourishes when the stars of tomorrow make their debuts today!

Revel in Jodi O'Donnell's STILL SWEET ON HIM—
Silhouette Romance #969
...as Callie Farrell's renovation of the family homestead leads her straight into the arms of teenage crush Drew Barnett!

Tingle with Carol Devine's BEAUTY AND THE BEASTMASTER—
Silhouette Desire #816
...as legal eagle Amanda Tarkington is carried off by wrestler Bram Masterson!

Thrill to Elyn Day's A BED OF ROSES—
Silhouette Special Edition #846
...as Dana Whitaker's body and soul are healed by sexy physical therapist Michael Gordon!

Believe when Kylie Brant's McLAIN'S LAW—
Silhouette Intimate Moments #528
...takes you into detective Connor McLain's life as he falls for psychic—and suspect—Michele Easton!

Catch the classics of tomorrow—*premiering* today—
only from ▼ *Silhouette*

Is your father a Fabulous Father?

Then enter him in Silhouette Romance's

"FATHER OF THE YEAR" Contest
and you can both win some great prizes! Look for contest details in the FABULOUS FATHER titles available in June, July and August...

ONE MAN'S VOW by Diana Whitney
Available in June

ACCIDENTAL DAD by Anne Peters
Available in July

INSTANT FATHER by Lucy Gordon
Available in August

Only from

SILHOUETTE® Desire®

DIANA PALMER IS BACK!

and bringing you two more wonderful stories filled with love, laughter and unforgettable passion. And this time, she's crossing lines....

In August, Silhouette Desire brings you NIGHT OF LOVE (#799)

Man of the Month Steven Ryker promised to steer clear of his ex-fiancée, Meg Shannon. but some promises were meant to be broken!

And in November, Silhouette Romance presents KING'S RANSOM (#971)

When a king in disguise is forced to hide out in Brianna Scott's tiny apartment, "too close for comfort" gets a whole new meaning!

Don't miss these wonderful stories from bestselling author DIANA PALMER. Only from Silhouette®

DPTITLES